CW01583446

Tommy's Girl

Part One

LAURA MORGAN

WARNING

Please note – This book is a thrilling crime story and is not suitable for those under 18 years old.

There are numerous severe triggers and intense scenes.

This book is dark. There will be moments you won't like and people you will hate. Know this before you go in...

ISBN-13: 9781980840787

DEDICATION

For Brian.
My Mr. Dark and Dangerous

ACKNOWLEDGMENTS

This book could never have happened without the superb help and advice from two wonderful ladies, Gemma and Sal. Without your guidance and support I might never have decided to go for it.

PROLOGUE

Piper

This is not a tale of romance or of love and passion with all the sweet and fluffy that comes along with it. This is a warning. A lesson.

There are two sides to my story.

Firstly, I fell in love with the most fiercely passionate and darkly obsessive man I'd ever met. He swept me off my feet and loved me so much he would do anything to make me his. It was wonderful in so many ways.

But, on the other hand, I also became the object of a monster's affections and paid the price for his love. I loved and hated it in equal measure, but learned one thing for sure.

I'll never be the same again…

If you're ready, follow me into the darkness. To where there is no light at the end of the tunnel.

Only Tommy, and the various sides to him.

***

Me? I'm a professional actress. I am allowed to say that because I went to drama school and because I was one of the lucky few who has made a living in 'Tinsel Town' as a full-time actor.

I have played almost all of the more modern roles out there in the various film industries and also put on a Victorian dress and recited Shakespeare like the best of them. I've donned a set of combats and trained my body hard in order to play an army girl in a zombie horror flick. I've mastered languages so I could speak them effectively in whatever movie required it, and I've learned to play more than a few musical instruments. I can even perform dances and martial arts to a decent degree. But really, I have always been given a role to play and lines to read, and that's it. I'd go out there and do it and somehow I've managed to do it well enough to keep being asked to come back and make more movies. Any actor's dream, I guess.

To be honest, I was happy with my modest fame and proud of my accomplishments. I'd not yet been the leading lady or the sexy starlet, but was okay with that…

Well, not really.

Don't get me wrong, it was what all actors wanted in the long term. To be the big name in bright lights. To be adored and screamed at by our stalker fans. Okay, maybe not quite that much, but I'd certainly had my share of fan boys and girls who made what I had accomplished all the more worth it. They were the ones who bought the movie theater tickets and DVDs, and if they kept wanting more, I endeavored to deliver it.

Things were going so well for me I could only hope it would continue. All that was missing was that coveted starring role to land at my feet along with the man of my dreams to sweep me off them. Yeah, a girl can dream, but in seriousness, the only thing I could imagine was me continuing my journey up the fabled ladder. If only I could find the right role to push me into proper stardom. To cement me in the halls of fame forevermore.

The only way I knew how was to take on something out of my comfort zone or to immerse myself in a role so deeply that I would transform for it—both mentally and physically. I wasn't sure I was ready to pile on the pounds for a role quite yet, but I did become intrigued by the extreme practices some people in my industry had studied. I began looking at the techniques outlined by the likes of Stanislavsky and his fully immersive methods, but wasn't sure I could be serious enough about the realism needed to properly do it any justice. I didn't fully understand how or why someone would want to perform in such a way. What did it add on-screen? How did it differ to what I'd normally done while starring in my roles?

I yearned to know more. To meet one of those strange creatures and study them. Learn their methods and try to implement it in my own work.

And then I met one and my entire world was turned upside-down. I can never forget when I got to work with a real method actor for the first time. Tommy Darke. He shattered everything I thought I knew about acting in a matter of days and proceeded to set about a sequence of events that would change my life forever.

For better or for worse…

ONE

Piper

I was getting ready to begin shooting my newest movie about a famous crime boss and his antics, set in the nineteen-twenties, when it began. Tommy Darke was the star. He was playing the role of George Ward, AKA 'The Boss.' I was playing the role of doting wife to a character named Ronnie who had been George's top henchman, played by the gorgeous Bradley Thomas.

Bradley and I had worked long hours together in the build up to shooting to ensure we had our roles fully hashed out. We'd get together and practice our lines while growing more confident with one another in readiness for the relationship we were getting ready to portray on the screen. It was going great and we both readily admitted that we had a natural chemistry I knew was going to work really well once shooting started.

We'd both been sure to attend the numerous workshops put together by the producers and of course the screen test shots in the run-up to filming, but every time the cast got together, Tommy was a no-show. We were warned not to expect an appearance, but every time we had one of the writers or producers step in to read his lines, it surprised me.

It became apparent I wasn't going to meet our leading man prior to shooting, but at the time I figured I wasn't that bothered. All I cared about was getting to grips with my own character, and then I could figure out how to work with the illustrious Mr. Darke. There were a couple of steamy scenes ahead for Brad and me that I'd have to get comfortable with, but mostly mine was the typical role of a woman of that era in her late twenties, even though I was much younger at only twenty-three. I was just another trophy wife. Playing the woman on Brad's character's arm while he carried out his work at the behest of his cold and ruthless mob boss.

In our sessions, I'd come to trust Brad and his ability to lead me through the given dialogue and scenes. I relied on him in the same way I did any other co-star I'd had in the past, but I like to think I also supported him, too. That he felt comfortable working with me.

There were some darker parts later in the movie I still had yet to work through, though. Scenes depicting when things started to break down for Tommy's character George, and even a sex-scene for him and me, and I had to wonder what it was going to be like working with him. I'd seen his photos and watched some scenes from a couple of his most recent movies in a bid to understand what I'd be working with, and there was no denying he was every inch the heartthrob who could pull off the role of gangster and loveable rogue with ease. But of course, he had his own way of doing things so hadn't so much as responded to one of my emails. I had no idea how, but I knew that with him as our leading man his method acting approach would dominate how the entire movie would be made and there was nothing myself, the other actors, or the production team could do other than tackle it one day at a time.

So, I arrived at the studio on the first day of shooting

and located Bradley and the other actors by the set. After greeting them all and introducing myself to the very few people I didn't already know—mostly smaller parts and extras as I'd made a point of reaching out to everyone I could beforehand—we got chatting, and that was when I was warned to expect the unexpected when it came to our leading man. I was right. Tommy had purposely stayed away in the build-up to our final run through, and I soon discovered why. He really was as his reputation had dictated. One of those strange but also renowned method actors. A rare breed of artist and I didn't know what to envisage. He had prepared intensely for the role and apparently believed he truly was George Ward the kingpin and head of the Ward family mob. A ruthless gangster and dirty dog, our lead character was about to embark on a journey of both incredible highs and epic lows before finding the error of his ways in the arms of the right woman, his leading lady. She was being played by the beautiful and up-and-coming new face in Hollywood, Scarlet Rosen. Based on real life events, we were about to portray the dark and intense story of a man at the top coming undone from the inside out. And Tommy was evidently going to live it for real. It was something I'd not yet experienced in the movie biz and had to admit, I was interested to see for myself.

We got to work and if I was honest, my initial opinion of him wasn't all that exciting. I didn't have much time with Tommy on or off screen at first, but while watching the first few scenes being shot, I couldn't deny he was beyond handsome. Inked up and stylish. Naturally rugged, no matter the shave and polish the makeup team gave him ready for the first shots, and his almost jet black hair was so thick and coarse I could make out every strand even from feet away.

Along with all the others, I watched him working through scene after scene, but couldn't fathom how there were fundamentally two men inside that skin. Tommy and George. Like a split personality or something, however for the purposes of the movie he was only letting George come out to play, and I quickly realized I had no idea who the real man was underneath.

My first scene with him was a couple days' in and I caved when it came to being positioned beneath that intense stare of his. Tommy scared me, but I used that fear to add an extra layer to my own character. Penny was based on the real woman who, as the story went, had put up with her drunken nobody of a husband for years. She never saw Ronnie because of his job within the Ward mob, and while my research had told me she was reportedly strong and didn't take any shit from the men around her, I also made her a little timid. I wanted her to be real to the women of my time but also of the days in which the movie was set. She had to be relatable. To be soft when she needed to be because she knew the men in her life wouldn't accept being treated like dirt by a woman. But then I knew she had also been ready to stand firm if the need arose.

Tommy's character George was confronting me in the scene. After being guilty of simply ending up in the wrong place at the wrong time, Penny had suffered the brunt of George's wrath whether she had earned it or not and had bitten her tongue rather than give him the lashing he'd deserved. As her bestselling biography had told it, this was the pivotal moment when things began to change between them, but at the time she had done what any other woman would've back when men ruled the world, especially men like George Ward. She'd caved.

Tommy was standing over me like some huge beast, glowering at me menacingly and I took it without batting an eye. I recited my lines as the script dictated and then backed off, just like I was supposed to. But, he wasn't satisfied. No matter the script, Tommy continued to stare me down, adding a sinister layer to the scene that soon had my knees trembling. By the time the director shouted 'cut,' he'd plucked a real reaction from me and I already knew this movie would be gold when shown on the big screen. Some things you just can't fake.

Tommy's gaze had penetrated me. Claimed me as his in some wild and feral way. I hadn't known why he'd done things that way until our next scene together.

For continuity purposes, we shot it right away while we were still wearing the same clothes etc. and so we moved sets and took our places. This was it, the scene when our characters were supposed to have a quickie in Penny and Bradley's kitchen. Following the script, I greeted Tommy at my fake doorway and pointed an angry finger at where Brad lay on the sofa, pretending to be asleep.

"He's passed out drunk, Mr. Ward. Nothing new there…" I said in my best Boston accent, before walking through the set of our apartment and George followed, closing the door behind him silently. "You wanna leave him a message I can relay for the mornin'?"

"No, let him rest. I came here for you," he answered, following me to the kitchenette like the script dictated. He was supposed to apologize for having been rude and give me a quick one while I bent over the counter, which is exactly what we played out before the numerous cameras and dozen onlookers. It wasn't hot, but the job was done as far as the storyline went because our particular quickie wasn't there to give the viewers rosy cheeks or a feast for the eyes. It was just one of many factors at the start of George's downfall. The moment that was to become the facilitator for his descent into chaos because, as the story went, poor Penny was to become pregnant with George's child.

As the crime history books told, the two of them had then hidden the truth from his one true love Josie, played by Scarlet, and from Penny's husband, but the secret would eventually eat George alive. The real George Ward then murdered his entire crew before slaughtering his wife and putting a gun in his own mouth. Penny's child was his sole heir and had then inherited her father's fortune before liquidizing his assets and disappearing, along with her mother's memoirs. She never resurfaced, but the story had. The writers had taken a softer approach to their movie though, opting for both Penny and Josie to survive his brutality, but it was still to become an intense tale of death and sorrow. Something they were all hoping the viewers would go wild for.

We did twelve takes in total and not once did we deviate from the script. Tommy hadn't allowed it for a start, and by the end of that afternoon, we had fake kissed and ever faker fucked our way into getting better acquainted. Not that it made me like him any more than I had earlier that morning. He was still a closed book to me.

And that was the story of how I met Tommy. Nothing too crazy or sexy. No explosion of heat and lust. Simply a work relationship like any other. If anything, I was kinda into Bradley back then and we'd hooked up more than just a few times while working on the movie. It isn't unusual for actors to fool around behind the scenes, and we were both single so weren't hurting anyone by it. Our liaisons were a bit of fun and the chance for me to blow off some steam with a hot guy, but I wasn't the type to fall head over heels with a co-worker so we would have our fun and then both saunter off casually afterward. A no strings kinda fling. Just how I liked it. I still remember with a smile how he snorted cocaine off my tits one night before eating me out like his life depended on it. Bradley was fun and boy did he like to fuck. (I guess I'll have to edit that part out before letting anyone hear this, but damn, he knew what he was doing in the bedroom all right.)

Now, back to the story at hand.

By the time the movie wrapped, so too had my fling with Bradley. There were no messy goodbyes. No spiteful, heated words. We simply stopped hooking up. Just another short-term fling that'd run its course. That was when I finally met Tommy. The real Tommy.

It was after midnight when someone came knocking on my door. I'd normally never even check it at that hour, but something made me go find out who could possibly be swinging by unannounced at that time of night. I lived in a secure area with guards and security and all that, so knew it shouldn't be some prankster or crazed fan.

Turned out it was Tommy. He told me he wanted to invite me to his house the following afternoon for a pool party. I was surprised by his invitation but accepted, intrigued to see the real him now that he was coming out the other side of his apparent immersion into the role of George.

I headed over there the next day and had assumed there'd be others there too, but got a shock when I discovered we were alone. It was a party for two and I wasn't impressed. As much as he was charming and had seemingly fallen back in touch with his real self, I knew it'd take me a while to feel comfortable around him. To forget the character he had been portraying the entire time I'd known him and see the real man beneath the cold and intimidating façade.

"What am I doing here?" I asked, but he simply grinned and stalked back inside his huge home. Like the curious little lamb I hadn't actually thought I was, I couldn't resist following. I wanted to figure him out and knew this was my chance. Tommy led me out into the garden to where his enclosed terrace overlooked the City of Angels. Man, he had an amazing view. I was instantly jealous but did my best not to let it show. He'd earned it, after all.

"I need to detox. To cleanse myself of George," he told me, stripping down to his underwear by the pool. "I was hoping you could help me?" With a bend of his waist, his boxers were on the ground along with the rest of his clothes and Tommy stood there before me in all his naked glory.

He had the typical movie star body with plenty of incredibly defined muscle and hardly any hair. His impressive cock was stood to attention, but I pointedly ignored it. I wasn't there just to be another quick fuck and then leave. Or was I? I couldn't remember why I'd even said yes to coming to his house, let alone having ended up stood there before the naked Adonis if it weren't exactly for that reason. But I didn't want him to assume anything of me.

Tommy then dived into the pool and I found myself stripping off as well before joining him. For some reason we didn't get right down to the dirty deed I'd clearly been summoned to his home for. Instead, we swam and floated in his perfectly clear and temperate pool, laughing and letting a strangely natural banter start to fly between us both.

He was funny. Far funnier than I'd picked up on during our filming, but I knew then how it was the real Tommy coming back through. By laughing and joking together he was indeed detoxing. Ridding himself of the extreme role he'd lived and breathed during the few months previously and it was actually an honor to behold. Something I'd never understood and yet I could see the transition with my own eyes.

After our swim, we then headed for the hot tub where Tommy offered me champagne and I readily accepted. He had some too, and we sat there with all our jiggly bits bouncing around thanks to the bubbles and making us laugh even harder.

"Who are you, Tommy Darke? The real you?" I asked him, sipping on my wine.

"I'm every character I've ever played all rolled into one," he answered with a sly smile. I giggled and shook my head. That wasn't enough and we both knew it. "It's true. They're all still a part of me, somewhere deep down. But mostly, I'm the real me. They just exist in the one percent of my brain that lets them."

"Like voices in your head?" I teased, but my smile dropped when Tommy fixed me with a cold and hard stare. One that both terrified and excited me at the same time. As if I'd just hit the nail right on the head. He then shook off whatever emotion I'd stimulated in him and took a deep breath, as though steadying himself. I had to wonder if anyone had asked him those types of questions before. If anyone had wanted to know the real him, rather than just bed the star and go on their way with an epic story to tell their friends.

"No, not voices. They're more like urges. Parts of myself I opened up when I played each of the roles and then had to lock away again. Pleasures and forbidden desires I never knew I had until I was forced to tame them again."

"Well," I answered, sliding closer to him with a sultry smile. "If it's that hard, how about you don't tame them, within reason of course? Just make sure they don't rule you. Learn how to own them while enjoying the spoils each forbidden desire brings you…"

Tommy's eyes flashed and his nostrils flared like I might've angered him by my comment, but he didn't say another word. Instead, he kissed me like he had no other choice but to have me. As though something else was driving him, something I myself had conjured within him. And, by God was it the most intense and memorable kiss I'd ever had. Our on-screen ones were nothing in comparison to this. Not even partway close. I lost all comprehension of time and space in his caress. I didn't swoon or go all girlie, but I did lose myself in him. It was unlike anything I'd ever known before. Like he was claiming me. Owning me. But, it was also like I owned him too.

When we finally pulled away, Tommy stared at me like he was suddenly terrified. He backed away and I took the hint, feeling oddly the same. Neither of us was interested in something big springing to life between us. We'd only been after a hook-up, but that kiss had been something else entirely.

I should've realized it when we'd spent the better part of an afternoon laughing and getting to know each other rather than letting off steam with a healthy game of hide the sausage. What was I thinking getting close to him and talking about the deep and meaningful? It scared me too and I backed off just like Tommy had done.

I then climbed out of the hot tub and made some lame excuse about having to get home, and was glad when Tommy didn't try and stop me. He watched my every move though and the desperate look on his face confused the hell out of me. I wanted to stay and sleep with him, but I had a feeling we would end up making love or some shit like that, and I wasn't prepared for it. Not in the slightest. The only time I had ever been in love before I had ended up with a broken heart and a lifetime of baggage. I wouldn't even talk about those days any more, or the girl I had been while timidly following around the love of my life like some lovesick puppy. That person was long gone and I was glad I'd come out the other side. Even a few years on, I had days when I crumbled. When I didn't feel strong enough, or when I heard his voice going round and around in my head telling me I wasn't good enough to become a proper actress. That I'd never make it.

So, like the modern day woman I was, I threw my clothes back on and walked away, trying my best not to let it show how what'd happened mortified me. I drove straight home and took a hot shower, where I relieved some of the pressure Tommy had stirred in my core, but it wasn't sufficient. I needed to properly unwind and playing with my clit in the shower just wasn't cutting it.

After drying off, I poured a large glass of wine from the bottle I thankfully already had chilled to perfection in my fridge and then headed back to my bedroom, where I watched some porn and drank my wine while getting down and dirty with my eight inch dildo. It sorted me out nicely enough and I fell asleep feeling far more relaxed than if I'd tried to ignore those needs. Plus, I wasn't ashamed to partake in some self-loving when the need arose.

The life and times of the rich and famous, hey? Well, I could've done something foolish like heading to a club and finding someone to scratch that itch for me. However, those stories almost always made the news and I wasn't that kind of girl, at least not as far as my public persona went. I had worked hard to maintain my girl-next-door image and was squeaky clean, so I was determined for it to stay that way.

I slept late the following morning, dreaming of that kiss, and had to repeat my chosen method of release I'd used the night before, minus the wine and the porn. I didn't need it anyway. All I had to do was close my eyes and I could see Tommy there in all his glory. I came with him at the forefront of my mind over and over, cursing myself each time I did, but then going back for more regardless.

My manager, Janie, came over mid-morning to check in with me and I soon got back to my normal routine of taking the calls she'd vetted and her giving me the options for my next possible ventures. I was quite particular in not wanting to get pigeonholed in the movie industry, hence my variety of roles in the past, so I was pleased to find a bit of all sorts in her bag for me to browse. There was everything from an upcoming Western to a voiceover spot on an animated movie. I picked out a few I liked the idea of and agreed to take a look at the scripts over the few days that followed and let her know if I wanted an audition arranging.

Janie was great. She had been a lifesaver in the past and had shown me how much I could be worth if I just played things the right way. I'd still been auditioning for advertisements when she'd taken me on as a client, but now I had scripts being regularly sent my way in the hopes I would come on board. I had friends in the movie industry who trusted me to be professional and trustworthy with their characters. They recommended me to their producer buddies and directors often asked for me to go and read for them. Life was good. Great in fact, and it was thanks to her in a lot of ways.

I was ready for my dreams to become an even bigger reality. All I needed now was that one big role. The chance to be the leading lady at last and hit the big time.

"Sure, I'll let Piper know. When do you need us back at the studio?" Janie's voice broke through my thoughtfulness. She was on the phone and I could see her making a note of something on her notepad. I didn't really have to ask what it was. Re-shoots were a common factor in filmmaking, but was surprised when my heart lurched at the prospect of being back in the same room as Tommy again.

Was I excited? No, of course not. Probably just anxious. "They need you back in at the end of the week for a few re-shoots," she confirmed once she'd ended the call and I nodded.

"Yeah, I figured as much," I replied, staring out the window at my back yard. I guessed I'd have to see him again sooner or later. We still had all the promotional work to do on *Wayward* yet, which would include us flying all around the world for the premiers and interviews together. Things would have to normalize between us or else it would show, so I decided I'd pretend if I had to. I certainly wouldn't let my afternoon with Tommy put me off my game.

"Are you okay, Piper?" Janie asked, and I turned to find her staring at me. I realized I must look a mess. Probably a little lost and too wrapped up in my own shit to carry on our usual conversation. That wasn't like me at all. I was usually proactive and my ambition pushed me to jump from one project right into the next, hence why she had turned up with some new material right after me finishing filming *Wayward*.

"Yeah, fine," I told her, snapping back to the matters at hand. "So, what are we doing today?" I asked, eager to get Tommy Darke out of my head by whatever means necessary, even if it meant working night and day to distract myself.

TWO

Tommy

I barely slept a wink after Piper left. I'd wanted her right from the moment I'd first laid eyes on her on set, but hadn't let George do the talking for me. It was one of my strictest self-imposed rules when it came to immersing myself in whatever role I'd taken on. It had to be me doing the talking when it came to personal matters, not my character. There had been times when I'd fucked my co-stars while still engrossed in whatever role I was in but it never truly felt like me. More like I was watching from the sidelines while the character I was in did the deed for me. I always ended up feeling dirty. Used by both the chick in question and my character. As if he had betrayed the trust I'd put in him when I allowed him to overtake my thoughts and actions. Yeah, I know, not crazy at all.

Not with Piper though. I'd waited until I was in the final stages of my comedown to approach her and she'd clearly been surprised to find me on her doorstep, but I couldn't blame her. It wasn't like we'd grown at all friendly while on set. When she'd come and stripped off at my poolside, I'd been sure we'd end up fucking in no time, but then she had made me laugh. She'd responded to my banter with her own and had drawn me further out of my shell. Made me want her for more than just that tight body I'd glimpsed more than just a few times whilst we'd been filming.

And then she'd taunted my dark side and something deep inside of me had salivated at the sheer idea of letting those forbidden desires come out to play. I'd almost caved. Those urges I always worked hard to quash had risen up at her command and when we'd kissed, it'd taken everything I had not to throw her over my shoulder and take her inside. Usually that wouldn't have been an issue, but not that day. I knew I wanted to do more than just fuck her. I'd imagined my hands around her wrists, pinning her down on my bed. My handprint on her ass after I'd spanked it raw. My cock pummeling her like some kind of battering ram and me not letting her leave until I was well and truly done with her…

Something told me she wouldn't have liked me all that much if I'd taken her body like that. She wasn't into that kinda thing. Not Piper. No, she wasn't like all of those other girls.

Or was she? Had I just not taken her hints? Damn, I was bouncing back and forth between the two assumptions and wasn't able to convince myself of either. Maybe she was like me? Good on the outside while all kinds of bad on the inside? She'd called to that part of me like she understood it. As if she had dabbled in those dark urges too. So maybe…

I knew I shouldn't have let her leave. I should have begged her to stay. Pleaded with her for one more chance. No scrap that, I'm definitely not the sort for the beg-and-plead routine. I should've downright demanded for her to take me the way she'd baited. Forced her to want me the way she'd made me believe she did.

Taken her every which way I desired whether she'd agreed or not…

There it was again, that darkness. It swelled and called to me so much stronger than ever. As though conjured from the depths of my soul at her command and now it haunted me. I couldn't rid myself of those thoughts, but I could ignore them. Yes, that was the right approach. I would ignore it all. The thoughts of Piper and her cute body. Those nipples as they'd bobbed on the bubbles in my Jacuzzi. That tight ass as she had sashayed away from me. So easy to forget…

"Damn it!" I screamed and I threw my coffee mug across the room. This wasn't me. I didn't obsess over women. Never in my thirty years had I ever been left feeling like this after a night with a woman. Especially not when we hadn't even fucked each other.

I got the call later that morning to say we had to go in for re-shoots and that was it. Whether she wanted to or not, I was going to show her who was boss. Who had and would always have the upper hand. Piper wasn't going to play me like some fool. She wasn't going to win. I was a winner in all things and this would be no different.

I would get back into character and do what needed to be done. And then, I would invite her back to my home and we would try the whole 'fancy a swim?' thing again. Next time, I'd have her spread eagled on the edge of my pool before she could so much as dip a toe in the water. I wouldn't wait. I wouldn't falter. I would take what I wanted and ask her to leave again, just like with all the other girls. I would do it to prove to myself how I was incapable of being ruled by a woman. To show I wasn't growing soft.

I spent the entire afternoon watching the interview tapes of George Ward I still had from when I was first becoming the man himself. It didn't take me long to get back into character because I wasn't fully out of it yet, but I enjoyed transforming back into the notorious mob boss. I remembered how I'd spent months learning his mannerisms and the inflections of his accent. But first, I'd researched his history. Plotted the timeframe and read every single biography there was on the man. I'd immersed myself in the world of gang culture and had spent days as a personal guest in one of Los Angeles's top gangs. My co-star, Scarlet had been my fixation for weeks in the run up to our filming. I'd sent her gifts and cryptic messages. I'd spent hours on the phone to her as George and she'd indulged me. I was positive she'd used my quirks to help get her better acquainted with the character too, and I knew for sure that by the time we'd started rolling, she and I already had the perfect connection. The right chemistry to portray the mobster and the woman he fell for. The one George put on a pedestal above all others. Even his own child.

THREE

Piper

I arrived back on set a little earlier than necessary and reacquainted myself with Penny over coffee with Bradley. It was strange how quickly you could disassociate yourself with a role once you were done filming and I always felt the same way when heading back for any extra shoots or retakes. I should've learned never to step away from the role until the director gave me the all clear, but something inside of me always seemed to switch off the moment we wrapped. Like I'd washed my hands with the person I'd been playing.

Usually I hated having to go back in, but this time, I found I didn't mind so much.

"There's only a few scenes for us to go over, Brad," I said, browsing through the notes I'd been given when I'd arrived. "Looks like we're getting naked again," I then teased, earning myself a salacious smile from my on-screen husband.

"Is that an invitation?" he asked with a wink.

I shook my head.

"Not today, big boy." I couldn't bring myself to tell

him why, but I wasn't interested in rekindling that flame, even if only for one last stoke. I still couldn't get Tommy off my mind and wanted to sort things out between us, but I knew there wouldn't be any of that yet. Tommy wouldn't be there with us, George would. He and I had to re-do our sex scene too but I didn't doubt for a moment that our heat wouldn't end up becoming a factor in the remaking of the scene. I knew I had to dull that fire in my belly for Tommy, to reduce the heat so that I could remain professional with George and not make a fool out of myself.

Yeah, it was going to be an easy few days.

After finishing up with the makeup lady, I tracked down the director, Bud, and asked him for a moment of his time.

"What's up, Piper?" he asked with a soft smile. I was glad he'd remained friendly throughout the filming process and I felt I could approach him, but I decided against blurting it out in front of everyone and ushered him to one side.

"I was just wondering if there was a problem with my sex scenes? I'm retaking two of them over the next few days and wanted to find out why?"

"Don't worry," he quickly replied. "I'm sorry, I thought it'd been explained already, but we've decided to make them a little steamier. The playback was ace, but we want more heat. To turn things up a notch."

"That would've been nice to know before now," I replied, but didn't dwell on it. These things happened. Bradley and I could do that, no problem, and I guessed I'd just have to play it however Tommy wanted to with the George and Penny scene. It wasn't like I could go and ask him to run it through with me.

"You'll do great," Bud told me, before stepping away to go and set up for the first retake of the day.

I could see Tommy across from me, his eyes on the ground as he paced in wait for the cameras to start rolling.

He and Bradley were about to punish a couple of George's dealers for losing some of his gear and I watched for a while as they filmed the scene again and again, getting the perfect angles and shots before eventually finishing up.

Bradley stayed bloody while Tommy wandered away and I was given the nod by the director to get in place.

"Baby, what the hell is going on?" I asked as I opened the door to our fake apartment and Bradley stumbled in, trying to wipe the blood from his face and hands rather than let me see.

"None of your business, Pen. Now, be a good little wifey and run me a bath would you?" he replied, shooing me away.

Penny saw red. I loved putting on my Boston accent and went for him, screaming and shouting as the script dictated about how he was the worst husband and I was so hard done by. Poor Penny. I actually felt for her, especially when Bradley turned on me, playing out the scene exactly as had been described in her memoirs. We'd both read the books based on her life countless times and rehearsed where we'd be and how we'd do it, and even I could tell we had some movie gold right there.

He pinned me to the wall with his hand around my throat, his face just inches away from mine and with a vicious scowl that had me quaking in my vintage boots. "Run me a bath and shut the hell up, or so help me God, I'll show you the back of my hand!"

"Sure thing, Ronnie," I replied in an icily calm tone I knew Penny had needed to perfect over the years or else take a beating off her darling husband.

Bradley cooled it with the threats and I sidled away when he finally let me go. "Take a load off and I'll go run you a bath, baby. Dinner's in the oven ready for 'ya when you've finished soaking." With tears in my eyes I then practically ran off set behind where our kitchenette would've been if it were a real apartment.

"Cut!" called the director and I looked up at Bud with

anticipation. "Nice one guys. That was perfect. Bradley, do not smudge or ruin your makeup. We'll go straight into the bath scene…"

We both did as we were told, waiting patiently while they set us up for our 'steamier' sex scene. Penny and Ronnie weren't the main couple of the story by a long shot, but they had their part to play in the mobster's story and I was ready to get down and dirty to make sure Bradley and I had our moment in the spotlight. I'd been working out like mad for months for this very eventuality. The first takes had only been timid portrayals of their lovemaking. My most nude scene had been with Tommy in the kitchen, but not after this, I was sure.

"You ready?" Brad asked with a wry smile.

"Always," I teased before following the makeup lady back to the chair so she could touch mine up just a little and make sure the tattoo on my shoulder was well hidden beneath the thick stage makeup.

When I returned, the set was ready and the team had just finished pouring hot water into a tub for Bradley to lie in.

"Action!" cried Bud and I watched from the sidelines as Bradley removed his bloody suit and climbed in the steaming hot bath. He showed plenty of ass as he lifted his leg over the side of the tub but then everything was once again hidden thanks to the strategically positioned bubbles.

I watched, waiting for my cue, as Bradley washed some of the grime away. He too had been working out and was flexed to perfection, and I was reminded again of the times we'd been together like this for real. There wasn't a thing wrong with the man as far as I could tell, but he still wasn't boyfriend material for me. I wondered if perhaps any one was. Nowadays monogamy was hard to come by simply because of a one worded question. Why? Why should we dedicate our lives to one person? Why should we struggle or settle. Why make do when you could have it all?

I was ushered on set and then sauntered over to where

Bradley was laying still half immersed in the tub. He had his head back and his eyes closed, and as the amended script had told me to, I kneeled down beside him and grabbed the washcloth, getting to work on scrubbing away the fake blood from his neck and chest.

"The doctor said there's no reason why I can't get pregnant, Ronnie," I whispered gently. "He said we're both young and healthy. All's we gotta do is keep fucking and it'll happen."

Quick as a flash, Bradley turned to me and his hand shot down my back and then over my ass. He lifted my dress and grabbed a handful of the cheek I had been holding tense at the ready.

"Hold it," the stage manager whispered and I knew they were taking a wide shot of Bradley and I in the preamble to our big scene. I began to pant gently, watching my 'husband' with a look that meant I was ready for him. "Okay, go. Slowly," we were ordered.

Bradley didn't need to be told twice. He grabbed the hem of dress and began to lift, revealing my panties and then waist, before finally reaching my chest when I leaned toward him. He then yanked the thin fabric over my head and tossed it to the ground.

He didn't say a word, but the scene was no longer what it'd once been. It wasn't Penny and Ronnie having a quickie, but a steamy scene portraying their love for one another despite his dangerous job and her carefree attitude that was going to get her in trouble later in the movie.

Following the stage manager's instructions, I then climbed up and into the water with Bradley, where I pretended to mount him. Thankfully, he'd kept his junk covered and I too had a flesh colored piece of material covering my bits so instead of riding him for real, I simulated the moves we'd done together time and again.

It took hours, but we finally got the right shots and eventually found ourselves standing in robes by the heaters for what we hoped was the final time of the day. The water had been topped up again and again with fresh warm suds, but I had to admit I'd had enough. I was wrinkly from the wet and cold in spite of the heaters.

I'd also ditched the cover that'd come unglued countless times in the water so was fully naked beneath my robe and surrounded by fifty or so crew members, but didn't care. They'd seen it all by now.

"We've got it," Bud informed the pair of us and I sighed in relief.

I turned to head back to my trailer, when Bradley stopped me with a gentle hand on my arm. He then leaned in close to whisper in my ear.

"Seeing as you've been writhing on top of me literally all day, how about we finish what we started…"

I fixed him with a scowl. There wasn't any part of me that wanted to jump back into bed with him, even if I'd enjoyed how many times I'd elicited a boner from him during the course of our afternoon in the tub together.

"Nice try," I replied, and knew I was being a tease, but I genuinely wasn't interested in going back there with him. I had other things on my mind. Or should that have been, other people?

FOUR

Tommy

I wasn't meant to stick around all afternoon, just do my few extra shots and then leave while the others did theirs, but I didn't. I stayed behind and watched them. Watched her. Piper. Penny… Whoever she was. I was drawn to her and had these intense urges. Like she belonged to me.

I stood in the shadows as Brad dared ask her to fuck him, but was pleased when she said no. She was mine now. Or she soon would be. We were filming together again the following day and I was more than ready to lay my claim on her as either George or Tommy, even if it was in front of an audience.

I followed her home that night. I couldn't help myself and stalked her as she walked inside her house and turned on the lights. Watched from the shadows as she made herself something to eat and poured a glass of wine. She seemed so relaxed and at ease with herself that I became even more enamored.

Did she know I was there? I didn't think so, but I couldn't be sure. Part of me thought she had to know and was toying with me on purpose. Either that or she wasn't very observant. How could she not have figured me out? How did she not know the extent of my need to own her? Could she really be that oblivious? No, she had to know. Had to be ignoring me on purpose because she was waiting too. Waiting for us to be together behind Ronnie's back. *Soon*, I promised her wordlessly. *Tomorrow*.

After just a few hours' sleep, I woke early and went for a run. I just so happened to pass by Piper's house on my way and I accidentally-on-purpose came to a stop so I could stretch out my legs and have a chug of water. I couldn't resist another peek into her home and slunk around the back to where I could see a light on inside.

Dear God. Not only was she already awake, but also, she was doing yoga. Yoga! Her body was twisting and stretching out right before my eyes and she was absolutely flawless. Utterly perfect. And all mine. I got hard within seconds of watching her and couldn't resist jerking off into her bushes. I left a piece of myself behind and she would never know it. She would never discover the secret voyeurism I'd started undertaking thanks to her.

Piper and her way with words that day in my tub had left me riled, and things had only gotten worse for me since.

She knows, a voice in my head chimed. *She saw you last night and has seen you now. She's ignoring you on purpose because she doesn't want you to know. You need to teach her a lesson. Show her you mean business. Force her…*

No, that couldn't be it. Piper had no idea of my presence, and even if she had caught me, I still believed she wouldn't tease me or ridicule me for it. No, not my Piper. She was perfect. Kind and sweet in ways I'd never known a woman could be. She was going to be mine. Whether that was George or Tommy talking I wasn't all that sure, but I knew it was true from both angles. She had two sides to her just like me, whether she realized or not. Her dark side had played with mine and now they were firm friends. Lifelong partners.

I arrived on set early and took my time getting dressed. George was meticulous in his grooming, and so was I. He always wore a crisp, tailored suit and tie, and so did I. When the makeup lady was ready for me, I watched my reflection rather than her. I saw myself transforming, delving back into myself and letting George take control once again.

Welcome back, George, I thought, smiling at my reflection.

"They're ready for you on set, Mr. Ward," the stage manager then told me, and I was pleased to see he remembered to address me properly. I didn't want to have to tell him off again like I had the first day of shooting.

Without a word, I followed him down the corridor to where a fake door awaited me. This side of the set was plain wood, but on the other side stood my prize. Her…

Knock, knock, I tapped gently on the wood and when it opened, I was greeted with the face of an angel. Her long blonde hair was tied up away from her face in a delicate knot and her pale blue eyes were dazzlingly beautiful thanks to the lighting on set, but I couldn't smile and greet her like something deep within me wanted to. I had to keep my scowl in place and deliver my lines. I had to play the bad boy first.

"Mr. Ward, what a surprise. Please come in," she said in greeting, ushering me inside her fake apartment. I did, but then hovered in wait for her to say more. Penny then pointed an angry finger at where my minion lay on the sofa, pretending to be asleep. "Ronnie's passed out drunk. Nothing new there… You wanna leave a message I can give him in the mornin'?"

"No, let him rest. I came here for you," I answered, following her through the living room to the kitchen like before. "I wanted to apologize for being rude earlier. It wasn't fair on you, Penny," I said, having to remind myself that was her name. I then leaned against the counter, watching her tidy up the fake dishes left on the sink.

"No need," she told me with a warm smile, which I then mirrored. I was supposed to bend her over the counter and have her while she was stacking the dishes, but I decided to do things a little differently. I'd been given creative license with the script thanks to my fully immersive ways so I used it to my advantage, adding a little improvisation to the scene.

"Something smells good," I replied, adding a sniff for good measure. Penny faltered for only a split second and then caught up quick. *Good girl*, I thought as she pointed to the refrigerator.

"Meatloaf and mashed potatoes. There's leftovers if you want some?"

"That'd be nice," I answered, and then watched as she plucked some fake food from the fridge and tossed it in the oven. Thank God for thorough assistants and set designers. They'd luckily had everything we needed already in place for continuity purposes.

Penny then bent over, giving me the perfect view of her ass as she continued to put the dishes away in a suspiciously low drawer. It was my cue again, and I didn't need to be told twice.

I reached forward, grabbed the hem of her dress and lifted, exposing the perfect, peachy curve of her ass. Penny let out a surprised yelp and stood up, which was when I pressed myself against her from behind and pinned her to the counter in front. I then pulled her to me, my hands around the tops of her arms. "Ronnie doesn't deserve you," I whispered in her ear, relishing in her compliance as she relaxed against me and placed her hands down on the worktop.

I was supposed to unbutton my fly and simulate sex with her from behind. I knew this. We'd done it numerous times during our other takes, but this time it was more than just the director's order to make things steamier spurring me to do things differently. It was that inner voice again. That desirous fiend who wanted more than he was meant to have. He wanted to rip off her clothes and force himself inside her sweet cunt. It didn't matter their audience, he would do it regardless and I was already hard just thinking about it.

Penny cried out again when I turned her to face me and she then peered up into my eyes like some sweet little doe. The lamb I was about to slaughter. The innocence I was about to defile.

"George?" she whimpered. I shushed her and then captured her mouth with mine. We'd kissed during our previous scenes, but never like this. I wanted it to be the kiss to end all kisses. The supreme and the sublime all wrapped into one. It wasn't because I loved her, but because I needed her. I had to make her feel for me the way I felt for her. To desire me the way I did her.

Penny gave herself to me entirely. I felt the switch happen in her as she succumbed to me not only for the sake of the movie, but in all things. And damn if that didn't make me harder.

After pushing her up onto the counter, I unbuckled my pants and lifted her dress up. There was no ignoring my boner so I concealed it beneath the layers of her skirt, hiding it for the sake of the censors while we acted as though I'd just slid myself inside of her. I rocked back and forth, feeling her heat through the cotton underwear that was the only barrier between us. Without that, I would've been in her for real and she knew it.

Focusing back on the task at hand, I simulated sex while our bodies mashed together for real. I wrapped her legs around me and kissed her hard, making Penny moan and pant like she was truly taking me deeper and deeper inside of her. God, I wanted to. When I pulled my lips away and watched her with a dark smile, I adored the flush of her cheeks and how her perfect makeup was now smudged. Her hands were on my chest, pushing me away while also holding me to her thanks to her fingers being curled around the lapels of my jacket. So wrong but so right.

I carried on, not knowing when, or if, I should stop, when she suddenly sucked in a breath and held it. Penny's eyes rolled back and she let out a sigh but was otherwise still. Well, except for the throbbing I could feel against the underside of my still thrusting cock.

She'd just come for me, I was sure of it. That was the hottest thing I'd ever experienced and it was only a second before I did the same. I spurted my jizz all over her stomach, still ever thankful for the dress keeping us covered from view of the cameras, and let out a groan for maximum effect. Whether the onlookers knew the truth or not, I didn't care. I played my part and acted like I was done. I didn't let her go though. I couldn't. Not after I'd just come all over her in front of twenty other guys.

Ding! Went the buzzer on the oven and I gazed down at Penny with a smile on my lips and a glint in my eye.

"Dinner's ready," I whispered, eliciting a genuine laugh from her.

"Cut!" called the director, breaking the silence from the crew all around us, and I was forced to release my grip on Penny's waist. Someone handed me a bunch of tissues and I wiped her clean, but didn't draw attention to any of it, and was glad when she didn't either. After tucking myself back in my pants, I then covered her up and helped her down off the counter.

She was mine now. I could see it in her eyes. She knew it too and I was pleased to see she wasn't planning on fighting it.

FIVE

Piper

Christ, what the hell was that? I thought, taking a moment to reacquaint myself with my surroundings. My legs were like jelly as Tommy helped me down off the counter we'd pretty much just dry humped one another over, but he remained the perfect gentleman as he waited for me to find my strength again. Had I really just had an orgasm live on set? Had he really just shot his load over me while the crew watched and the cameras still rolled? The answer to both those questions was a unquestionable yes.

I was mortified, but also walking on air. It'd felt amazing and we both knew it. I just hoped it looked as good as it'd felt. No one said a word to us as they rearranged the set in readiness for one extra scene Bud decided was going to be shot off the back of mine and Tommy's far steamier sex scene. I was glad for the few minutes to compose myself again, but I couldn't take my eyes off Tommy. Mostly because he couldn't seem to take his eyes off me either. He looked at me like he owned me. As if some deal had been made by our bodies in that moment and he expected me to follow through on it.

I realized it wasn't Tommy who had claimed me though, but George. He was still in character and had been the entire time, and that realization brought me back down from cloud nine in a heartbeat.

"I'm okay now, thanks," I said, side-stepping out of his hold. I then took a deep breath and walked away, and while Tommy looked disappointed, he let me. I could still feel him watching me as I headed to the refreshment table and downed a glass of water, but didn't mind. I guessed in his mind, he and I were lovers now. He'd soon snap out of it once the re-shoots were over again and we could go back to our normal lives. When we could forget all about our intense attraction as Penny and George.

"Stay exactly the way you are now," the stage manager called to me. "Bud wants you both back on set in the kitchen but sat at opposite ends of the dinner table. George will be finishing up with the meal and he's gonna say something like 'we should do this again sometime,' to which you'll agree. Got it?" he asked and I nodded.

We then acted out the scene as directed but kept it more or less improvised like we had the other scene. It worked somehow, and like I had before, I followed Tommy's lead.

Afterwards, we were sent off while they checked out the footage and were promised an answer within the hour as to whether they needed anything else. Rather than stay with the others, I spent the time on the phone with Janie in a bid to distract myself from the matter at hand. And the man ever present in my mind.

After lunch, Bud informed us he didn't need to do any more to the scene and I was glad. It wasn't that I hadn't enjoyed turning things up a notch, I just felt like we couldn't necessarily recreate it the same way so was glad we didn't have to start all over again. My body couldn't take it for a start! My clit was still a little raw from Tommy's rubbing while simultaneously also being swollen with the need to satisfy it with something more than a mere strum. Part of me wondered if Bradley was still around so I could take him up on his offer from the day before, but I knew that wasn't what I wanted. Not really.

I wanted Tommy. I'd tried to deny my feelings for him all week, but our session on set had cemented that desire for him inside of me. I'd seen him naked and in all his buff glory by his pool, but when I'd felt him push that thing against me, all my resolve had disappeared. If he asked me over again I knew I would say yes. I also knew I'd probably jump his bones the minute we got behind closed doors.

All I had to do was wait for him to come back out of character, however long that might take.

***

I spent the next few days in turmoil. I found myself waking up in the night fretting over the sex scene with Tommy. Had it ended up too erotic? Would it make me look bad? I began the age-old routine of becoming riddled with self-doubt and fear, and with an intensity to both I hadn't experienced for a long time. Not since my first few roles when I managed to convince myself I was a hack who didn't know what she was doing each and every damn time. I tried to tell myself it wasn't true. That the movie was going to be awesome and I had nothing to worry about, but I couldn't get away from that sinking feeling in my gut.

I knew what had me all over the place. Tommy Darke. I soon came to realize that it might be because he was one of the most amazing actors I've ever met and I felt like my own acting didn't stand up next to his. He didn't just put on a costume and recite lines. He becomes the character, inside and out. I'd heard of method actors before, but had no idea the depth of their role-playing until I'd worked with one for myself. Until he'd dragged me into the darkness with him…

Another week passed and I still hadn't heard from Tommy. I tried everything to distract myself but none of it was working. And to top it all off, I still couldn't sleep.

With a huff, I climbed out of bed and walked over to the window, peering down into my small yard below. I wasn't one for anything fancy, nor had I put much thought into renting my first home. All I'd needed was somewhere comfortable and safe. Home was where I kicked off my shoes, or so we'd always said. Deep down, I guessed I was still the army brat I'd been as a kid who could lay down roots wherever she went. I'd travelled the world with my parents and had recreated myself every time. Playing one role after another for as long as I could remember. I had been an actress my entire life, and it was no wonder I found it so natural now.

Something moved in the bush to the side of my house as I stared down while lost in thought, I was sure of it. I watched longer but saw nothing so pulled my nightshirt around myself. Maybe I was imagining things. It wasn't like I was completely with it the past few days or had slept well at all. No wonder my mind was starting to play tricks on me.

SIX

Tommy

That was close. What was she even doing awake at this hour? It's the middle of the night and she ought to be fast asleep. I knew I should be too, but that was beside the point. I was a delusional deviant with a serious case of obsessive-compulsive-attachment with a woman I hadn't even slept with. I was allowed to be skulking around her house in the dead of night. It's what crazy people did and I was pretty sure I was certifiable about now.

I was on the other side of the characterization and George was slowly slipping away, but this time he was clinging on for dear life. He didn't want to be locked back in his box and it was driving me insane.

Forcing myself to go home, I took a shower and shaved for the first time in days. I then popped a sedative and flung myself into bed. Sleep came, thank God, but it was filled with images of her. Of me taking her properly over that counter while everyone watched. She was telling me no while guiding me inside of her, playing coy when we all knew she wasn't.

I woke up with jizz all over my stomach and groaned.

How many times had that woman made me come? Far too many to count that was for sure, and still not once had that load been shot where it was supposed to. Her cunt was still a mystery to me and I was determined that wouldn't be the case for much longer.

When she left her house for the first time in days for a photo-shoot I knew the studio had lined up, I went back to my spot at the back of her house. There, I watched the house, lying in wait, and eventually it paid off. Her gardener came around the other side and opened the back door while he replenished the vases with flowers for her and then headed around to the front, leaving it wide open.

I took my moment of what I considered to be divine intervention and slipped inside without a sound.

I stayed hidden until the gardener had tidied the back yard and then locked up again. Once the coast was clear and the house was silent, I then wandered around, looking at all of Piper's things. Her bookshelf was bigger than her movie cabinet, which surprised me, and I plucked a few of the most tattered titles from the shelves. They weren't the classics I might've expected someone who was trying to show off to have on display, but contemporary romances and even some science fiction. I approved of her choices and took a huge hint from her pick of romantic novels. Alpha males and billionaire bad boys galore. Each domineering and determined to take the leading lady as theirs, no matter the cost. That had to be what she liked about them. Each book was like the last in that same way and I knew then and there how it wasn't going to be a case of waiting to get her out of my system. It was quite the opposite. I had to have her so much I would get bored. We all got bored in the end, there was truth to the saying 'too much of a good thing.' I would take and take and take, until I no longer wanted what she had to give me, and then I would walk away. Like the powerful men she fantasized about in her nightly reads, I would be forceful and courageous, while also showing her just enough of my softer side to let her believe I was still the good guy.

Was I the good guy? Really? I'd broken into Piper's home and was planning to have my way with her, use her up, and spit her back out again. That wasn't what good guys did.

George. I blamed George. Before him I was a happy go lucky type of guy. Our banter and fun in my pool and hot tub were testament to that. She was also partly to blame, given how she'd stirred my inner darkness and lured it out. Piper wanted it this way. That was why she'd seen right through my façade and how she could possibly know what was lurking beneath the surface.

After a good look around, I decided to hide out in her guest room until she came home and then I'd surprise her. Probably scare the hell out of her too, but I hoped she was game. I needed her to be, otherwise things were going to get weird pretty quickly.

I laid down on the bed and closed my eyes, thinking about all the things Piper and I were going to do to each other. That was all well and good, but then whaddya know, the lack of sleep caught up with me and the next thing I knew, it was nighttime. Thankfully, with me having been hiding in her guest room, I hadn't been spotted, but I could hear her a few doors away. She was humming to herself as she climbed into bed and I cracked open the door, watching her from across the dark hall.

Piper was wearing just shorts and a cami. Her tits were on full display, nipples tight like rocks she was smuggling under her skimpy top. I longed to caress them but froze rather than step out of my hiding spot to go to her. She wasn't going to be flattered by my presence. She was going to be furious. I'd made a huge mistake in staying and regret washed over me. I could go to jail for what I'd done. She could ruin not only my life but also my career if she called the police.

When Piper then went into her en-suite, I took my

chance to leave and scurried towards the stairwell.

I was halfway down them when I heard it. A sound that immediately stopped me in my tracks and had me turning back around. Before I could second-guess myself I was climbing the stairs and walking into her bedroom. I approached the bathroom door and pressed my ear to it, my eyes closing as the sound washed over me. She was crying. Soft sobs permeated the wooden door and invaded me one hitched breath at a time. I loathed that sound and suddenly wanted to make it stop by any means necessary.

I didn't know what to do. Should I run from her tears like I had with everyone before? No, I wanted to hurt whoever was responsible for them. To punch their face into mush. But, what if the culprit was me? Hadn't I already suffered enough because of her?

I was so lost in the sound that when it suddenly stopped and the door was wrenched open, I forgot I was an intruder. I opened my eyes and watched as Piper jumped out of her skin and then began screaming, and all the while I was just stood there wondering what on earth could have her so afraid. That was when realization struck. I was the reason.

"Shit!" I cried, lifting my hands in a bid to tell her I meant no harm. "Please don't call the cops."

Piper suddenly stopped screaming and scowled at me like I'd shocked her more by my response than my presence in her room in the dead of night.

This was good. Better she be angry than afraid. Now, I just had to win her over and then we could get back to the real matter at hand. Me getting what I came for.

SEVEN

Piper

I opened and closed my mouth, undecided as to how to respond. I knew I should kick him out. That I ought to call the cops and the press, in fact call everybody and out him as the twisted pervert he clearly was if he was skulking around my house uninvited in the middle of the night. I wanted to be furious with him for invading my privacy, but I wasn't. I was oddly flattered.

Just moments before I'd been feeling so sorry for myself I'd actually had a good cry. I'd convinced myself I was unloved, uncared for, and unwanted. I'd felt lonely beyond anything I'd experienced in a long time and while the rational part of my brain knew it was just my insecurities still flaring up, I couldn't seem to convince myself those vile thoughts weren't true.

But then I'd opened the door and found Tommy standing on the other side. I think I'd shocked him as much as he had done with me, but I couldn't laugh about it. In fact, I still hadn't reacted at all, other than my initial screams in surprise.

Rather than tell him to leave or threaten him with

prosecution like my brain was telling me I ought to, I decided to follow the urge in my belly instead. The need that'd been growing and growing in spite of my regular use of my battery-operated boyfriend. The desire to have him, once and for all. To have a night of passion like I'd been dreaming non-stop about.

I stepped forward, tentatively at first, but then I flung myself at him. Tommy was more than ready for me, and I was glad. He'd come into my home uninvited and we both knew why. I knew what he wanted and was more than ready to give him it.

He tore away my clothes and threw me on the bed, where I watched as he too tossed off every inch of clothing he had on and then lunged for me. He was rough and aggressive with me, and I loved every second of it. His kisses weren't delicate or full of gentle care. They were hard and consuming, as if he didn't want me to breathe. Or at least, he wanted to take charge of every inch of my body including my basic functions and needs, so let me take breaths as and when he allowed it. I gasped and found myself lifting up on the bed, unable to take it any longer for fear of passing out, which was when he grabbed my hips to stop my escape and plunged inside of me with that rock hard rod between his muscular thighs.

I arched my back and caught my breath at last, and then could do nothing but lay back in euphoric ecstasy as he pounded into me over and over. He didn't seem to care for anything other than claiming me, but damn, I wanted him to. I never wanted it to end, even when I came for him, and thankfully he didn't.

Tommy knew I was coming, but he didn't so much as slow for me to recover and carry on. He continued to slam into me over and over again and it never even occurred to me to tell him to stop.

We carried on that way for hours. Tommy was a relentless lover and I had a feeling he too had a lot of pent up attraction for me he'd been trying to fight. Something that'd come to overwhelm us both but thankfully we'd been able to finally exorcise some of those demons via a night of passion, albeit thanks only to him violating my privacy.

When we were both finally spent and my body was screaming at me to let it rest, I looked over at Tommy and took him in. He was beautiful, even with his obscure urges still swirling within him. I could see it behind his eyes, but foolishly wasn't scared. In fact, I think that was what I liked about him. He had a dark side. A dangerous edge that had me both terrified and tantalized all at once.

I checked the clock and it was almost dawn. Shit. I figured this could go one of two ways now. We could snuggle and fall asleep in one another's arms, and then wake up a few hours later to talk things through and figure out where our night of passion was going to take us. Or, we could go the other way. We could continue our 'no strings' affair and otherwise not draw attention to the wild nights of passion we'd hopefully enjoy together time and again in the days to come. I opted for the latter, not being the sort to want a relationship of all the gooey lovey stuff, so rather than nestle myself in Tommy's arms, I climbed out of bed and plucked his clothes up off the bedroom floor.

"Here," I handed them to him, and found myself relishing in his surprise. "Time for you to go home, Tommy. Be sure and lock up on your way out," I told him, before disappearing into my en-suite for a hot shower. By the time I emerged, he had indeed gone, and a wide smile spread across my face as I climbed back into bed and nestled into the sheets that still smelled of him. Of us. I was asleep in an instant and had the best few hours' rest I'd had in weeks.

I was up and doing my late-morning workout when my cell went off. I'd just finished a wobbly tree pose, given my overall tiredness and the tenderness of my core, and so welcomed the chance to take a break. Hitting speaker, I grabbed my water bottle and took a swig while Janie's assistant connected our call.

"I hope you're ready, Piper?" she chimed through the loudspeaker on my handset.

"For what?" I asked with a frown.

"To conquer the world, of course!" she squealed, making me laugh. I was glad to hear she hadn't meant anything else, and forced my anxiety away. For a moment there all sorts of things had whizzed through my head. Had Tommy been spotted leaving my house? Had someone found out about us and blabbed to the press? I liked our liaison being a secret and wanted it to stay that way.

"What are you talking about?" I groaned as I wandered over to my living room window and peered down into the garden below. I had to stifle a gasp when I saw who was waiting for me down below, spying on me from the bushes. So I had been right the other night. Someone had been there. He wasn't even trying to hide this time. He'd been watching me again and wanted for me to know. To catch him in the act like I had the night before. My heart beat wildly in my chest but I refused to so much as grin at him or register his presence in any way.

"The director loves the new scenes, babe. He rang this morning and said the first round of edits are amazing. Your chemistry with Tommy is apparently off the charts!"

I hummed in answer, thinking how if only she knew the half of it she might actually be speechless for once.

"That's great. However, I'll believe it when I see it," I told her, but couldn't fight my smile. I was shifting. Growing. And it was all thanks to Tommy. Whether this thing between us went anywhere or not, I didn't care, because I somehow knew that my life was about to change. "Did he say when we could watch a copy?"

"Not for a while yet, but he does need you in today for more photos. They've decided to do some extra promos with you as a featured character, not only Scarlet," Janie replied, and I could hear the smile in her voice. This was good. Great, in fact. I wasn't the leading lady and yet I was being given extra limelight thanks to my on-screen performance. This could be the opportunity I'd been waiting my whole career for. The chance to get noticed by more of the right kinds of people. Those who could make my dreams come true by offering me a follow-up role as the star, or at least the co-star of my next movie.

Yes, I was getting ahead of myself, but it wasn't impossible to believe in it happening. All I had to do now was keep my reputation as a professional and trustworthy actress intact. I would be on time for every meeting I was asked to attend. I would work hard and do everything I could to make *Wayward* a success. And when it was, I would bask in my limelight knowing I'd earned it. That I deserved the recognition afforded to me and then humbly accept an upcoming role as leading lady by those who had only considered me a supporting actress in the past.

"We need to make sure this works," I replied, knowing how Janie would understand exactly where I was coming from. What elevated me also benefited her in the long run too and I knew she was as big of a shark as any other agent in Los Angeles. She would fight tooth and nail for me if I asked her to.

"Oh, don't worry, sweetie. I'm gonna make it my mission to have your name everywhere people look. Your face on every poster. Just watch me…"

"Looking forward to it," I told her, and then changed the subject. I was eager to get off the call and back to my workout, only of a different kind. "When do they want me?"

I put my cell on the table and stared down into Tommy's eyes. We really were heading into dangerous territory, but I couldn't stop myself. I wanted to celebrate in the only way my body was craving. I pulled off my tight yoga top to give him full view of my then naked breasts.

"I spoke with Sarah who's the photographer's assistant, and she said sometime this afternoon. They haven't been able to get hold of Tommy yet as he needs to be there too." I smiled again, thinking if only she knew he was standing just a few yards away from me. But I wasn't going to reveal all. In fact, the longer he remained unreachable the better, because that meant I got to have him all to myself.

"Okay, just send me a text with the time and place and I'll be there," I said as I removed my pants and underwear, standing fully naked just inches away from my window so I was on full show to my voyeur.

"Sure, I'll let you know," Janie answered and then she ended the call. I continued to stand there for a few seconds and then I went straight to the back door, which I opened a crack and stalked away again.

I then bounded up the stairs and jumped straight in yet another shower, needing to be clean rather than sweaty from my workout before Janie's call.

When the cubicle was suddenly full, the body of my tall and broad lover blocking out the light from overhead, I began to tremble. He was silent, but gave off a vibe so dangerous I had to consider whether what I was doing was even safe, let alone a good idea or not.

Tommy was coming out of a deep characterization that made him unstable and unpredictable, and I was egging him on. I was nurturing those dark edges of his personality rather than helping him extinguish them. He was meant to be detoxing, but instead he was stalking me. Lurking in the bushes. Breaking into my home. Fucking me like he wanted to both hurt and pleasure me, but as if he didn't know which one was the stronger of the two urges. And what was worse was that I was letting him do it rather than get Tommy the help he might actually need. He took me from behind this time, parting my thighs and lifting me onto him while pressing me into the cold tile wall. My pussy screamed at first, stinging a little from our escapades the night before, but once he started to move, I was putty in his hands. Tommy kissed my neck and then licked his way down over my shoulder before nipping me with his teeth. I felt my body clench around him with the shock of his bite. It wasn't hard enough to leave a mark, but it was enough to make me squirm in surprise.

Tommy cursed and I wasn't sure why, but then I felt him pulsating inside of me and knew. I'd elicited an orgasm from him with my movement and I don't think he liked it. I think he wanted to control when and how he came undone thanks to me because it gave him the power. But not this time.

He withdrew and let his release wash away down the drain. I thought he was gonna put me down so we could dry off and head to the bedroom to start all over again, but instead he spun me around to face him and then dived back in. His kisses on my lips were as forceful as they had been the night before. But this time, I was clever. In spite of the water rushing down over us from above, I moved against him and took my breaths when I needed them, rather than when Tommy allowed it, and I knew he didn't like it. He liked holding my life in his hands.

When I was ready to come, he reached up and took my chin in his huge hand, forcing me to keep my mouth on his. He wasn't going to let me go, not even when I was crying out with my explosive climax, and I knew it was his way of regaining his control. Taking the power back. When we were done, Tommy put me down, tilted his head up, and let the water cascade over his glorious body. He let me watch for just a moment. To take a mental picture, and then—just like that—he was gone.

A quick dry off and he was out the door, not needing to be told to leave this time. He went of his own accord, and by God did I enjoy watching him walk away, because we both knew this was far from over.

He'd be back again and our power play would continue, whether either of us liked it or not.

EIGHT

Tommy

My thoughts were running wild as I slunk out the back door and around the back of her house in my usual way. I was becoming far too comfortable with sneaking around Piper's property and it scared me, but what terrified me the most was how far I was willing to take all of this. At first, I'd tried the 'normal' way of getting her attention, but I knew how things with her would never be normal. I couldn't stand it. Not after everything we'd shared these past few days.

I'd tried to walk away but then my affection had come bounding back during our on-screen exploits. I'd somehow managed to convince myself it'd been an obsession borne out of our character's liaison, and I'd been so wrong I almost had to laugh. It wasn't George who was obsessed with Penny. It was Tommy and he had an ever-ready hard-on for all things Piper. There was nothing I could do and, so far at least, no amount of times I could fuck that obsession with her away.

She pushed my buttons. Poked the hornet's nest deep in my soul. Piper had welcomed me into her bed but she hadn't submitted to me for even a moment. No matter how hard I'd been, she'd wanted it harder. It didn't matter that I'd left her close to asphyxiation, she'd taken it without so much as a fight.

She was challenging me and I'd be damned if I didn't rise to her enticement. But, I was going to win. I always did. Piper had no idea how far I was willing to go with this. How deep my need for her was becoming. I could feel it scratching at my soul, making holes the shape of claw marks in the walls I'd built around my heart and the darkness I knew was also in there. It was seeping out, slithering to the surface.

I was going back to her house that night. I'd already decided on it before she gave me a strip show and literally opened the door and let me in. To be honest, it didn't matter whether she let me in or not, I was going back there whenever I damn well pleased. And I didn't need for her to open the door as I could do so myself thanks to the extra key now hanging on the chain in my pocket. I'd stolen her door key on my way out in the early hours when she'd dismissed me rather than let me share her bed any longer. That'd been as sexy as hell I had to admit, but she'd issued me with yet another challenge, and one I'd readily accepted. Getting the key cut was a doddle. Then it was back to her place to lie in wait for her to take a shower so I could put it back again, and the rest, as they say, is history. I'd put the key back on my way up to her room, still grinning at how she'd left the door open for me in invitation anyway.

Was I under her skin as much as she was under mine? Yes. I had to be, otherwise there was no way she would continue with such a strange charade.

There was a buzzing sound that grew louder as I approached my car, which reminded how I'd thrown my cell in the glove box before heading to the house a couple hours' earlier. I had a ton of missed calls and messages, but deleted them all and sped away. An over exaggeration, maybe, but I wasn't interested in what anyone had to say. There was one thing I had to do before I could head back to reality. One stop I had to make so I could stock up on some essentials for when I went back to her. For when I made sure she knew who was boss in this little tryst of ours.

My cell rang again, being sent to my car stereo via Bluetooth and I answered with a bark.

"Finally! Where have you been, man?" my assistant, Miles, asked.

"Fuck you, Miles. Just tell me what's going on," I replied. I wasn't going to tell him shit and we both knew it. He'd been my assistant for years and had suffered through every one of my intense ups and downs. Like the time when I disappeared for two weeks and turned up at his apartment looking and smelling like a junkie. I'd been living in a crack den the entire time and while I'd chosen not to get high myself, I'd watched the others and documented the stages of both their highs and lows. I'd watched people hire out their ass for crack, or worse, their disease-ridden cunts. There was no way I wanted any part of that, but when the time came to shoot the movie I'd been prepping for, I was more than ready to portray a man living from one hit to the next.

"They need you down the set this afternoon. They're shooting some pictures for promos and first up it's you and Scarlet, followed by you and Piper." Just hearing him say her name made me want to curse at him. He wasn't worthy enough to say it.

What the actual fuck was the matter with me? I shook it off and focused back on the matter at hand.

"Tell them I'll be there in an hour," I ordered him and then ended the call. There was plenty of time for me to get to the store and back before heading to the set. But still, I pressed harder on the gas and saw my knuckles turn white against the black leather wheel as I tore off towards my destination.

NINE

Piper

After a midday nap, I awoke to my cell chiming on my bedside cabinet and found the timings for my afternoon on set. Janie was going to send a car for me in an hour, which was great. It gave me time to straighten my unruly hair that was now fuzzy from being washed and left to air dry twice in just a few hours.

I also applied some light makeup and pulled on a figure-hugging dress I knew any paparazzi at the studio would be pleased to get some nice shots of, but that would provide nothing revealing or embarrassing to the image I was still so determined to keep wholesome. My tan was perfect, as was my waxing, thanks to my regular visits to the beauty salon, so I made myself a coffee and relaxed while I waited for the doorbell to chime.

I smiled to myself as I sipped on my hot drink and wondered what Tommy was doing. Was he turning on the charm with Scarlet or was he struggling, having to imagine me in her place so he could portray the devotion to her he was meant to? I hoped it was the latter, and when the driver knocked on my door, I greeted him with a wide smile and left the house with a spring in my step.

I arrived on set within a half hour and headed right on in, not needing or wanting any chaperones or direction. All I wanted was my chance to take the perfect photo with Tommy. My chance to shine and bask in some of his limelight while establishing my own.

While our fantastic artist Deana was still making me up, Scarlet came in and began changing into her own clothes, a sign they were finished with their photo-shoot. I almost asked her how it went, but didn't want to seem too eager, so simply offered her a smile when I caught her eye in the mirror.

"He's not as weird as he was while we were filming, but there's definitely something strange about that guy," Scarlet told me as she tied her sandals and then stood, smoothing her skirt and checking in the mirror that she looked presentable.

"Thanks, I'll be sure and handle him as best I can," I replied in a way that I hoped was non-committal and that also didn't show just how ready I was to be under Tommy's hard stare again. "Are they going with the dark and brooding shots?" I had to ask, and Scarlet nodded.

"Yeah. Don't think I saw him smile once," she said with a giggle, before giving me a wave and strutting off without another word.

I began to feel nervous. What was he going to be like? Would he be the man I'd let into my home for a stalkerish booty call not once but twice now? Or would he back in character? Did George await me in the studio, and if so, what on earth would he think of me?

There I went again, acting like George was a real person, or at least as if he was someone other than Tommy. The same Tommy I had been fantasizing about day and night. That had to mean I fancied George too?

I was damned if I could figure it out.

Instead, once Deana had worked her magic and I was wearing my finest vintage style dress, I pulled up my proverbial big girl panties and took a deep breath before pushing through the door that led to the studio where the camera had been set up.

I veered straight for the group of assistants and nodded to one of the runners I'd met the day before while shooting with Bradley.

"What's the plan?" I asked, feeling awkward all of a sudden.

"Tommy's just having his makeup touched up and then we're good to go. The photographer will direct you where and how to stand," she replied, which I could've already guessed, but at least she gave me something to do for thirty seconds. I was on edge and liable to start a random conversation with any passer by just to fill the time if I wasn't careful, so instead I walked over to where a plain black background covered the floor and wall. There, I waited patiently to get started and tried not to look too uncomfortable in the process.

I sensed him before I saw him. That sounds so cheesy but it's true. I honestly felt the air shift and the room suddenly fell silent. I remained rooted to the spot, staring at nothing yet I couldn't tear my eyes away. I just knew he was going to have me in the palm of his hand the moment I peered into his eyes and wanted to fight it a moment longer.

Shit. I was falling. Not in love, but in lust. I was caving to every desirous thought running through my usually so sensible mind but I couldn't stop myself from carrying on. I didn't want to.

"You're going to do everything I say, Piper. Is that understood?" his deep, husky voice penetrated me from just inches away from my left ear. I didn't know how he hoped to achieve such dominance given the way these photo-shoots usually went, but I was willing to give it a try. I'd never been the submissive type, however there was something about Tommy's intense sensual side that made me want to do as he commanded. To follow his orders and be his willing slave.

"Yes," I replied, almost silently.

"Good, now turn to the camera and show them what they want to see so we can get out of here." I did as he asked and found the team all silently watching us from behind the photographer and the numerous lighting umbrellas that'd been set up around the small space Tommy and I were stood in.

I was surprised to find the man behind the camera standing in relative quiet. Instead of telling us what to do and where to position ourselves, he instead gave Tommy a nod and then began snapping away. "Straight face. Stare down the lens. Pretend it's the day when I shouted at you. Remember how horrible I was…" it was Tommy giving the orders and ultimately, I wasn't surprised. He had an affinity for this stuff. Knowledge not learned or passed on by some wise mage, but instilled in him through experience and a natural connection with the camera.

I followed his lead and did exactly as he'd said, straightening my face so that I could widen my eyes in fear. The snap, snap of the camera didn't distract me, but Tommy's closeness did. He was pressed against my back, his lips at my ear, and my breath hitched when his arms reached around and grabbed me around the waist. His hand rested over my stomach and I knew exactly where he was heading with his direction.

I placed my own hand over his instinctively and closed my eyes, smiling ever so slightly. I imagined I was really Penny. How I was pregnant with a child that wasn't my husband's and yet still had to hope that things could work out all right for us.

Before I could think about our next move, Tommy had my hair in his fist and he'd used his hold to turn my face up to his. I opened my eyes and finally caught a glimpse of him. Not George, but Tommy. He was there this time and he was peering down into my eyes like a man possessed. On a mission to rule all or else lay waste to it rather than let someone else win.

"Excellent," said the photographer, still snapping away. "Hold it there and if you can give us a tear, Piper, that'd be great." He shifted position and began capturing our moment again. Tommy nodded in agreement with the order and I summoned my tears on command, like all good actors could do. I let my eyes well and then blinked, releasing the perfect droplet down onto my cheek, where it rested for a moment before sliding down to my chin and then fell.

"I don't like watching you cry, Piper," Tommy then told me, and it came as a shock. Part of me had taken him for a probable sadist. One who wanted to dominate me violently using pain as well as pleasure. But then I thought about it properly. He hadn't hurt me, even while being a forceful lover. He hadn't spanked my backside like men had in the past or so much as pinched my nipples during our frolicking in the bedroom and then in the shower. His bite had been like it was more about shocking me rather than delivering me pain and it was a realization I welcomed.

I felt myself curl into Tommy's hold. Wanting him to squeeze me tighter because I trusted that he wouldn't hurt me. At least not physically. I had no idea how or why, but I had the distinct feeling he was about to mess me up in ways I would never see coming. Some of those forbidden urges of his he'd shown me were all about power play and control. He had to control me, or at least it seemed that way, and against all my better instincts, I wanted to let him.

We continued for a short while, but it felt like formality more than anything else. Covering all the bases set by Bud, but we both knew they'd got the perfect shots already. And what they didn't have the team of graphic designers could easily merge together from a shot that was right. Even I knew I didn't naturally look as good as I did in the photographs created for movie promos and such. It was a given in this industry that the airbrush option was everyone's best friend.

When we were done, I stepped out of Tommy's grasp but he pulled me back to him, pressing my back against his torso. My gaze shot around the room, checking who might be watching, but everyone was going about their business and paying us no mind. They each wanted to get home as well no doubt so weren't watching what we were doing, and I figured Tommy had known that when he'd yanked me back into his hold. "This is how this is going to work, Piper. When I speak, you listen. When I call, you come to me. Do I make myself clear?"

I wanted to tell him no. To go to hell and to shove his demands up his ass. But I didn't. Instead, I peered back over my shoulder at him and grinned. He wasn't going to get it that easily.

"Are you forgetting who it is you're talking to? I'm the woman who kicked you out this morning because I don't need hugs or kisses, or to fall at a man's feet to feel worthy. I don't need you to love me, all I need is for you to give me what I want," I told him, stepping away. "I'll listen. I might even come to you, but I'll do it on my terms, Tommy. Are we clear?"

He didn't say a word or move a muscle. No nod of approval or laugh of dismay at my apparent gall. No reaction at all. I wasn't going to beg or plead with him for one either, so I carried on walking away. I didn't need him playing games or calling the shots. I was stronger than that, and so I didn't so much as look back as I stalked off set.

I hit the dressing room and ditched my clothes, threw on my dress and sunglasses, grabbed my purse, and left the studio like nothing had even happened.

TEN

Tommy

I spent the drive up to the cabin in fits of both rage and laughter. The old me, or I guess the 'normal' me, found it funny that Piper and I could have such a strange and fascinating way about us. I loved the back and forth. The hunger we each had for the other, and yet the reluctance both of us had when it came to backing down. I found her entertaining in both a sexually gratifying way and because she amused me in general. I enjoyed her laugh and her smile. I wanted to make love to her all night long and also make her scream in ecstasy.

I also liked watching her, even as she'd gone about her normal business, just… well, because.

And then there was the other part of me. A side of myself I was slowly beginning to get to know. One I had kept locked away for so long I'd forgotten how it felt to let him out. To let him be free.

Becoming George had been the key to opening the door and yet it was Piper who had taken his hand and yanked him back into existence. That both scary and exciting part of myself found her an amusing plaything. It wanted to have all of her until she had nothing left, and all the while craving nothing but her complete submission.

I had begun to obsess over her. To need her to want to give me everything and for her to give it willingly. To downright insist upon it. I knew there was also an undeniable urge in me to fuck her raw and watch her scream in anguish and beg for me to stop.

But not cry. Never cry.

Tears made me remember the reason I had locked that part of myself away for so long. Made me remember the tears that had broken me so long before. Seeing her cry would mean I'd done a bad thing again and I couldn't have that. I'd only barely come away unscathed the last time and I couldn't allow history to repeat itself. Not after I'd been so careful to turn my life around and bury that particular past. I knew I had to tell her, but not the full story.

Only how it was my one rule. My one necessity.

I arrived at my destination and charged inside, where I took my purchases from a couple hours' earlier and arranged them on the kitchen counter. I'd fantasized about this for so long, but never with someone specific in the role of the female. Not until Piper had come charging into my world and encouraged me to indulge in those fantasies. The unusual and, I guess, slightly depraved urges of mine. And now she was going to pay for it.

After everything was ready, I opened the curtains over the large bay window to reveal the glorious sunset, and the reason I'd bought the cabin in the first place. The San Gabriel Mountains had been the perfect choice of venue for my escapes to the woods. I could hunt and hike to my heart's content, or use it as a sanctuary where I could come to drink myself numb and play computer games or loud music all night and no one could hear me. No one even knew I was out there half the time, and the same would be for Piper once I let her into my secluded secret. The only difference was that for her visit, we wouldn't be playing games or listening to music.

Plus, there was only one thing I wanted to hunt.

Her.

And I was ready to receive her,

I took a photograph of my sunlit balcony and attached it to a text message on my cell.

Tommy:

I want you here with me, Piper. I don't care what plans you might have made or what bed you thought you'd be in tonight. Come to me. And clear your schedule, what I have in store for you will take more than just one night…

I added the address and hit send. And then the nerves set in. Would she come? Did she want to spend time with me the way I anticipated she would? I damn well hoped so, otherwise I knew she'd see my bad side in one way or another whether she wanted to anymore or not. The connection we'd shared so far had been intense and she'd peered right into my soul. She had seen the real me and hadn't run from him. In fact, she'd invited him in over and over again.

She'd let me watch her. Let me fuck her. Not forced me away when I'd snuck into her home and violated her personal space. Those moments simply couldn't be undone.

The sound of my cell vibrating on the counter startled me and I lunged for it. She was calling. Not texting back, but calling me, and I had to take a breath before answering.

"I'll be there by ten," she said, before I then heard a beep that signaled the end of the call. Yes. She'd chosen to be a good girl after all.

Everything was falling into place perfectly, so now all I had to do was wait.

ELEVEN

Piper

I arrived at the address Tommy had given me thanks only to my trusty navigation system. I'd never been up into the San Gabriel Mountains before but couldn't deny they were certainly beautiful. After parking beside his truck and cutting the engine I took a moment to gather myself and have a look around.

The cabin seemed quaint but well kept, as though Tommy had someone who looked after it for him while he was home in Los Angeles, and I could see the balcony where he had to have taken the photo of the sunset.

The house was built on the mountainside itself and from this angle I could see that beneath the viewing area were great huge stilts holding it up amidst the trees. They looked sturdy enough, but I still cringed at the idea of stepping out onto it. I hoped I wouldn't feel too scared to walk out onto the wooden platform if asked to. I wasn't all that great with heights but thought how nice it'd be if I managed to watch the sunset the following day there. Preferably with a glass of wine in one hand and Tommy sat beside me.

I flushed hot in anticipation and wondered what awaited me inside. Was he going to try and dominate me? If so, would I let him? I didn't think I could, and had failed in my attempts at being a submissive lover in the past, but he hadn't seemed that way. Tommy was downright paradoxical really and I struggled to get to the bottom of his likes and dislikes when it came to the real him in real situations. He'd not hurt me and had said himself how he didn't like seeing me cry on set. Perhaps he was the submissive one and I would need to learn how to be a dominatrix for him? Maybe he wanted me to be the one to elicit whatever pain or pleasure he needed? Possibly it was neither. Not every relationship had to have a dominant and a submissive after all. It stood to reason I was just another of the sexually explorative women my age who assumed everyone had to have a label. It made things easier in the bedroom, yes, but in my experience it was sometimes less exciting too. Lacking the surprise and the intrigue.

Tommy certainly had a lot of both of those though, and as I walked up the steps to the large wooden door, I found myself growing desperate in my need to see what awaited me on the other side.

He answered it without me needing to knock, as if he'd been waiting, watching me, and I enjoyed the idea of it. Like when he'd been skulking around in my garden, watching me like a man obsessed. I'd enjoyed that too. I'd liked having his eyes on me and had gotten off on knowing he was watching me so intently.

Tommy didn't say a word as he led the way inside via a huge, open plan living space and over to where a table sat in front of a bay window. He simply sat down at the head of the table and continued watching me as I ditched my jacket and overnight bag I'd come prepared with.

"What do you want me to do to you, Piper?" his voice thrummed through the air and hit me like a wall of heat. Damn, he was hot. Just the sound of his voice had me weak at the knees and I didn't have to think twice about my answer.

I didn't falter, nor did I hesitate. I knew exactly what I wanted and wasn't afraid to tell him so.

"I want you to fuck me, Tommy. Like we did at my house last night and this morning. I want more of what we had together," I replied as I turned and wandered over to him.

He looked sheepish, as if I'd caught him off guard, and I cringed. Maybe that wasn't what he'd wanted to hear, but then why had he summoned me to his cabin in the woods? We weren't particularly well acquainted with cuddling or having a date night. The only real interactions we'd had thus far had either been in character or through hot and steamy carnality.

"I don't want that," he finally murmured with a scowl. I stopped in my tracks and gripped the back of the chair I had been about to pull out so I could sit down beside him.

Oh great, I thought. He'd brought me here to call things off between us and I'd just gone and made things one hundred times more awkward. Tommy didn't want me. And why would he? I was a fool to think someone like him would be interested in me.

Yep, there I went with the shame spiral and the self-doubt. It'd been kicking my ass a lot recently and it reared its ugly head again just when I thought I'd gotten over it.

Angry tears pricked at my eyes and I turned away. I wasn't going to give him the satisfaction of knowing he'd hurt me. My nerves were shot and I wanted out of there before Tommy could hurt me any more. It was like my old boyfriend all over again. Before he could break me like he had.

"Fine, I guess I'll see you around," I replied, and was almost back to my bag when I heard his chair screech across the wooden floor. Before I could look back, he was on me. Tommy's hands were wrapped around me from behind and one was clasped around my throat, pulling me back into him.

I let out a yelp, surprised by his outburst.

"See, this is why I'm fucked in the head. Too messed up to be trusted with you, Piper," he growled in my ear. "Before you I was happy to fuck every which way I wanted and then leave. I was satisfied with everyday girls and their everyday cunts."

"But not anymore?" I choked back, my breath hitching thanks to his hold.

"No, not anymore," Tommy replied. "I wanted to see you hurting just then. I enjoyed watching the regret and shame cross your face when you thought I didn't want you. I've had those kinds of urges my entire life but have never felt close to giving into them. Not until you reached into my soul and played with my demons. Not until you brought them to the surface and made them feel special."

"When?" I asked through my hoarse breaths thanks to his hand that was still wrapped around my throat. "How did I do that? By not freaking out when I found you in my house, or was it when I caught you lurking around in my back yard?"

Tommy sucked in a breath on a hiss, his hold tightening ever so slightly.

"Way, way earlier than that, Piper," he whispered in my ear in answer. "I'm talking about that night in my hot tub when you stared into my eyes and told me it was okay to give in. To let those urges rule me. And I did. I am…"

"And ever since that night, what have I been to you? An experiment? A test to see how you like letting your dark side out?" I asked, and then spun to face him.

Damn, he looked amazing. The cheeky party boy I'd met that night by his pool truly was no more. He had something wild in his eyes. Something dangerous. And he was right. I liked it.

"You're becoming more like an obsession. When I look at you I don't see another girl for me to have my fun with. Far from it," Tommy answered, eyeing me up and down with those intense blue eyes of his. "There are two sides of me warring inside. One part wants to punish and torment you for the sheer thrill of it. It's like I need to see you suffer, Piper, but not because I want you to be in pain. I want it because, well, I want to be the one who makes it better. The person who licks your wounds and takes care of you afterwards."

"That's rather perverse, don't you think?" I said after taking a deep breath, trying not to show how much his words had gotten to me. "You want to be both my tormentor and my protector?"

Tommy's eyes dropped to the ground and I had my first taste of what it felt like to do exactly what he had described—hurt him for the fun of it. But unlike him, I wasn't going to leave him thinking I wasn't interested in exploring the desires spurring to life inside of him.

It wasn't a fantasy of mine to see him hurting. I wanted him to soothe my pain, not for me to have to help him overcome his own, so I put an end to his suffering and grinned from ear to ear. "It's a good thing I'm a sucker for the perverse, isn't it?"

TWELVE

Tommy

Damn, that woman was sure making me work hard to get her where I wanted her. But, like the deviant I was, I couldn't resist her lure. I was enjoying the up and down. The back and forth. It was exactly what I'd wanted from a potential relationship with the only person who had ever made me want more than just a quick fling. Most of the time women were lucky if they lasted more than a night, but with her, I wanted forever.

"I'll tell you how I envision this going and you can stop me at any time to negotiate, okay?" I asked and she nodded but said nothing while the black pools of her eyes swallowed me whole as she awaited my proposal.

I was a glutton for punishment and waited, watching her a moment longer. Waiting to see if I saw any flicker of doubt on her perfect face. There wasn't any, only that continued immense stare. I don't think she so much as blinked.

I felt smothered by her. Like I couldn't breathe, but also as if I no longer wanted to. "All of this will stay between just you and I. Neither of us want anyone knowing what's going on behind closed doors, but I'm happy for us to eventually be outed as a couple should this play out the way I hope it will," I said, relishing in the flush of her cheeks when I mentioned how I was up for more with her. For us to be a real couple.

I surprised myself by actually wanting it too, but reminded my wildly beating heart that it was still early days. We were in lust, not in love. This flame could burn out just as quickly as it'd ignited. "I want to make you squirm, Piper. To see you suffer and to humiliate you for my own enjoyment. I plan on tying you up and having my way with you however I see fit. I want to make you my slave. My whore. A prize only I am allowed to enjoy because you're too terrified to so much as look at another man, let alone allow him between your legs."

"You cannot leave a mark," she interjected and I nodded. Our livelihoods counted on us being perfect and screen-ready at all times. It wasn't an issue. I'd already planned how I could be careful not to mark or scar her. To keep Piper's body in the perfect, pristine condition it currently was.

"Of course," I told her. "I'll ensure that you're safe from any lasting harm, because that's the nature of this beast within me. like I said, I also need to protect you and to care for you. I'll save you from… me. I'll make you feel on top of the world again and then some, because that's where you belong, Piper."

"You promise?" she whispered and I saw real fear in her eyes. Someone had made her feel bad before. Had humiliated and tortured her, but unlike me, he hadn't made it all better again afterwards. He hadn't taken away the bad and replaced it with so much goodness Piper had left his company feeling cared for. Feeling loved. She looked as if she might cry and I recoiled, being reminded of my one condition. My only hard limit, so to speak.

"I promise," I said, making sure my voice was calm and even. "You have to trust me just like I will have to trust you. Rely on me implicitly to take what I need and then flip the switch inside of me so that I can give you what you need, Piper. The sex you spoke of, yes, but also much, much more than that. A connection. Perhaps even more." I stepped forward and took her hands in mine, kissing each palm tenderly. "I do, however, have one condition."

Her stunning eyes peered up into mine, and I could tell she was searching for something. Trying to guess what it was her self and I loved how she was trying to figure me out. Trying to get there first without me having to lead her to my truth, but she could never guess what'd happened to me years before. There was no way she would figure out the reason behind my need to both punish and protect, or my reasons for never wanting to see tears streaming down her pretty face.

"What is it, Tommy?" Piper eventually asked me, taking my mind away from the memories of my youth and the girl who had once ruined me.

"Don't ever cry, Piper. Never. If you do, the moment's over. There will be no making it better and no taking it back. It's my only trigger." She didn't actually seem all that shocked and I wondered if I had given too much away earlier at the photo-shoot when I'd told her how much I'd hated seeing her cry. Luckily, I was still ever so slightly in George mode, otherwise it would've been days before I could've seen her again. Maybe longer. Even knowing they'd been fake tears had still churned my stomach and I guessed she'd somehow been able to tell how much it'd affected me.

Not wanting to go into any other detail on the subject, I turned the conversation back to the matter at hand. My proposed indulgence in all the things my immoral and devious side demanded in return for her well-earned aftercare. "Do you think you can do it? Give yourself to me? I want you to play a role for me. Become my captive, here in this cabin. Give me the chance to explore these desires of mine and then we can go from there. Continue on together…"

Piper seemed a little hesitant and part of me wanted to get down on my knees and beg, but I simply couldn't allow myself to do it. I needed her to say yes all on her own. Not coerce her. She had to be mine. Not only in the sexual sense but in every way I could imagine. I had impulses only she could help me explore. Urges she had summoned that demanded she say yes otherwise I wasn't against forcing her to stay. Making her see sense.

"Only if you promise me," she eventually whispered, stilling my frenzied mind. "Promise you won't hurt me, Tommy. Promise you won't take me for granted or leave me behind. I need to trust you before we can venture too far into the unknown, but it'll take time so we need to go slow. I need to know you'll let me be what you need in my own time. That you won't get bored of me."

Oh bless her heart. My darling girl. So naïve and timid. How could I ever tire of her?

"I'll never get bored of you, Piper. Don't you see? I'd fix whatever's broken inside of you before I could ever break it any more. I promise," I reassured her, and like that, I saw the decision to submit to me fill Piper's eyes before she even told me her finite yes.

This was going to be fun.

THIRTEEN

Piper

What the hell was I thinking? Tommy wasn't only completely inexperienced with this whole 'unleashing your inner desires' nonsense, but he was clearly using me as his test subject. It could all end seriously badly, and yet, I stepped closer to him.

I said yes.

And then I let him strip me naked and cuff me to his bed.

He'd at least thought things through, or so it seemed. He'd bought the Velcro cuffs with thick banding so it wouldn't cut into my skin. There was bottled water by the bed and the sheets had been freshly laundered. They were soft, as though ready to be slept on, rather than any of the awful deeds I'd imagined as Tommy finished preparing me and then climbed back on the bed to admire his handiwork. I thought he might say something, but he didn't, all he did was stare as he sat cross-legged on the end of the bed. I waited for whatever suffering he had planned for me, but he continued to do nothing at all. Nothing but stare.

Time passed slowly and I eventually began to grow cold and tired of waiting. Impatient. I tugged on the cuffs, lifting myself higher on the mattress, but there was no give, so I twisted my arm in a bid to loosen it. Nothing.

Tommy grinned up at me from his position at my feet and his smile was so wide it reminded me of a comic book villain. Or at the least some kind of voyeur who chose to say so much through saying nothing at all. I watched him lean closer, his fingers rubbing his bottom lip as he saw my skin pucker like gooseflesh thanks to the chill.

In the minutes that followed I went through a wide range of emotions. I'd initially felt excited and somewhat scared of what he had planned, but was rapidly growing bored of his game. My boredom quickly turned to impatience and then frustration.

"What are you waiting for?" I eventually demanded, throwing a kick in his direction and missing, which only served to make me angrier. "Come on, Tommy. You said you wanted to watch me suffer, so make me suffer! Get it over with."

He turned and straightened his legs before climbing up off the bed, where he began pacing up and down, his eyes still glued to me. "Is this it? Is this your super plan? You're going to bore me to death?"

Tommy burst out laughing and I thought for a moment he might shrug his shoulders and tell me he'd been wrong. That after trying out his whole thing out he'd come to realize he wasn't cut out for it after all. But no.

He didn't come and untie me. He still didn't say a word. And he didn't hurry things up. I let out a disgruntled cry, surprising myself at how angry he was making me.

Like a petulant child not getting her own way, I then proceeded to throw a strop and even when it got me nowhere I carried on, spewing profanities the likes I'd never said before. I was cold, bored, tired and angry. My mouth was dry, reminding me of the water just inches away, but when I told Tommy I was thirsty, he did nothing. With that wild smile and a look in his eye that meant business, he simply continued to watch me squirm and I began to realize what he was doing.

I was suffering. Not through pain or anything dramatic, but through my basic needs for warmth and nourishment having been taken away. He was starting slow. Like he'd said, I was now his captive. He decided when I ate and drank, not me. Tommy would decide when to warm me up and cover my naked body with a blanket or some clothes and I knew nothing I said or did would affect his decision.

"Tell me what you need, Piper. How do you feel?" he asked when I'd finally calmed down and was laid on the bed, staring back at him with a scowl.

"I feel vulnerable. Tired. Thirsty." I curled my legs up against my torso as best I could to try and get some warmth back into them. "And I've come to realize I don't like being tied up."

"Why?" he asked as he grabbed my feet and yanked my legs back down. Tommy then climbed over me and I instinctively curled up against him in spite of him having tormented me, desperate for his warmth.

"Tell me it's over now, Tommy. Please," I replied, but he shook his head.

"It's not over until I see how much you're willing to suffer to please me, Piper. You don't like being tied up, why?" he asked again and I let out a huff.

"Because it kinda makes me feel claustrophobic, if that makes sense? As if I'm trapped, and I don't like it," I answered, trembling beneath him regardless of the heat he was sharing with me.

"And why do you feel vulnerable?" he demanded as he climbed back and shoved open my legs, giving him full view of my pussy. Normally I wouldn't mind, but he wasn't doing it to make me feel desired or wanted. He wanted to push me to my limits before the switch could be flipped and instead of feeling sexy, it felt all sorts of wrong.

I found myself wanting to get there sooner than later. Wanting this part to be over with so I could get to the good stuff.

"Because you aren't looking at my naked body as though you want to pleasure me. You're looking at me like you want to torture me," I replied, trying to pull them closed again, but he wouldn't let me. Tommy pressed down hard on my thighs, reacting to me exactly the way I'd expected. I decided to take things to the next level. To force him to go there whether he was ready or not, just like he was doing with me. "Get your fucking hands off me. I'm done with your games and I'm done with you, Tommy."

My words lit a fire within him I could see shining from the windows to his soul—his eyes. Something snapped in him and it was my turn to grin as I watched Tommy struggle with how to handle my rejection.

With a growl, Tommy thrust two fingers inside of me and I cried out, writhing against him like a woman possessed. It was wetter than I would've thought after being more angry than turned on by his antics so far, but I couldn't deny his touch had me warmed up and desperate for more in a heartbeat.

"I say when you're done, Piper," he informed me, stroking his way in and out a few more times. "And it's not yet," Tommy added, removing himself and climbing up off the bed again.

I let out a garbled cry. I wanted to tell him I was sorry and beg him to come back and finish what he had started, but I knew this was all part of the game. It wasn't time to move on from the punishment side of things yet, so with a groan I snapped my legs closed and cursed at him.

Tommy continued his routine of torturing and then pleasuring me until I was fit to burst with all my denied orgasms. When he finally flipped that damn switch of his and thrust his cock inside of me, I exploded in seconds. It was too much. Too bad and yet so good I had the best and most intense climax of my life.

"I hate you," I teased as I came down from my high and Tommy didn't reply. He simply unbound me and then lifted me into his arms before carrying me into the bathroom where a steaming hot shower awaited me.

It felt so good to get warm again, especially when Tommy lathered me up and began washing me. Taking care of me like he had promised. Bringing me comfort and a sense of accomplishment for what I had given him.

"Let me look after you," he groaned, his hands running over my soaked skin while his eyes were closed. Like he was in some sort of daze. "Let me make love to you now, Piper. I need you to know how gentle and giving I can be."

I wanted that more than anything. We each rinsed off the last of the soap and I shut off the shower. Tommy then followed me back into the bedroom, each of us dripping wet, but we didn't care.

"Show me," was all I said as I climbed back onto the bed he'd tied me to and pulled the covers up over myself in a bid to stay warm. Tommy joined me and then he did exactly as he'd promised. He made love to me.

FOURTEEN

Tommy

I awoke the next morning with a human hot water bottle draped over my chest, but I didn't care one little bit. For the first time, I didn't want to sneak away and then make a run for it. I wanted to stay and hold her. To watch her sleep and greet her the moment she finally woke up.

She hadn't denied me one thing and even though we really had started slowly, she'd seen me for everything I truly was and hadn't run either. After me letting my fear stop me from indulging for so long, I'd finally opened up to someone and she hadn't laughed at me or called me a freak. She had said yes. She'd let me torment her for my own pleasure and had reacted just how I'd hoped, even when she hated unleashing her usually so controlled anger.

That'd been my true undoing. Knowing I had the power to make or break her in those moments was exhilarating. To be able to unravel Piper's very many layers of calm and controlled exterior was a power I'd craved, and now I had it. I could've untied her at any point and apologized. Let her walk away. But I hadn't. And most importantly, she hadn't given up on me. Piper had trusted in me to deliver on my promises and I'd been morally bound to finish what I'd started. I'd adhered to the rules and flipped that switch when the right moment had presented itself.

It'd been perfect. She'd been perfect.

There would always be a part of me that craved more though. I could've watched her squirm all night. Seen her rage and scream. Watch her beg… damn, now that would've driven me over the edge. I might never have let her go if she'd turned fully submissive on me, but then again, that wasn't really what I wanted. I'd had a hundred women who had fallen at my feet and treated me like a God, but not Piper. She fought me every step of the way and I adored it. I always had liked a woman with a good deal of attitude about her. I already wanted to take things to the next level. Like an addict, she had given me a high I craved more of, but I knew I had to fight my urges at least a little. I couldn't let them get the better of me. I ruled them, and not the other way around. I had to remember that. Piper stirred and let out a soft hum in her sleep. She was adorable. Too adorable. But I reminded myself how the cute little lady lying next to me wasn't cute or adorable at all. She was a slut who had let me fuck her anyway I'd desired. She hadn't cared while I'd defiled her with my filth.

"Whore," I whispered to her. "You're such a fucking whore, Piper. I'm gonna show you what I do to whores…" she was still asleep as I positioned myself behind her, the tip of my cock at just the right angle to take her again. I parted her lips, dipping my head inside.

"Not now, Tommy," she whispered groggily, pulling away just enough so that I was no longer nestled in the perfect spot. I felt like grabbing her and plunging myself inside, whether she consented or not. Like having my way no matter the consequences, but instead, I backed off. I did the right thing.

My good side won—this time.

FIFTEEN

Piper

I woke the next morning with the most amazing feeling in my belly. I felt, I don't know, happy? I certainly felt wonderful, put it that way, and knew it was Tommy who had helped make me feel that way. He'd let me rage on him when we'd been playing his game of the predator and his prey and I had loved letting all my frustrations go. I hadn't held back. For the first time in forever I'd let my words fly without a care for being the good girl. It'd felt good to offload my rage and I couldn't deny there was a huge part of me wanted more of it.

Tommy woke up not long after me and he was beyond attentive to my every need. He made me breakfast and then we fooled around for a bit, which was lovely. I giggled and played coy while he teased me and bargained me into submission. We were acting like teenagers again and I was walking on air, until he suggested we take a dip in the hot tub. This was my nightmare. I desperately wanted to join him, but the tub was out on that horrible deck and my fear of heights came crashing down on me like a suffocating haze.

I went over to the glass door and looked out. I could see through the tiny gaps in the floorboards and down onto the forest below. They looked far from safe and I was convinced they would break beneath my feet and I'd fall.

"How about a walk instead?" I suggested, trying my best to sound aloof. I wasn't sure he bought it, but Tommy agreed and then he grabbed us some supplies while I used the bathroom and got freshened up.

By the time I was dressed and good to go, he had the truck packed and indicated for me to jump in the passenger's side. I looked into the cab and pouted. "What happened to our walk?" I demanded, and he simply shook his head in response before jumping into the driver's seat and starting the engine.

I climbed in and fastened my belt, figuring we were still having fun after all, so I decided to be adventurous and I let him decide our next step. Tommy sped away and at the end of the long drive that led to his cabin, instead of turning right for the highway, he turned left, taking us further up towards the mountain's peaks.

After a few minutes, he then turned down a dirt track and I had to grab the handrail above me to stop from flying around in my seat. I giggled, watching him drive, and he couldn't hide his smile even though he was concentrating hard on the road ahead.

Tommy was dazzling, a true movie star, and I was smitten with him. I knew it.

When we came to a stop and he put the truck in park, I climbed out of my seat and over the center console so I could straddle him. He knew what I was after and his pants were around his thighs and his cock free and pointing up at me before I could even get out of my clothes. He knew exactly what to do and with a grunt he had me down on him the second he'd spied that my underwear was out of the way.

I let out a garbled cry and tried to move, but there was no way he was going to let me take control and ride him.

Not the ever present dominant force that was Tommy Darke. With my legs tangled thanks to my ineptitude at getting my pants off, he used them to hold me in place while he thrust up inside of me again and again.

It was heaven. Like a jackhammer pummeling up and into me over and over, while I was pinned against his steering wheel and could do nothing but lean back and take it as he fucked me hard. It felt exhilarating to let him take me like that. Like I was an adventurous teenager again and we were parked up in the woods for some naughty alone time.

I loved it. The truck smelled like real forest pine and the windows were steamed up just like in the movies. My senses were all heightened and every element of it just added to my euphoric ecstasy.

Tommy was soon grunting while I was letting out those weird noises that were something between a groan and an, 'oh my God,' but neither of us cared what we sounded like. All we cared about was being together.

When I came, Tommy started pounding me harder. I figured he must be close and that was why, but when he didn't stop and I came a second time and saw the wicked smile on his face, I knew why he'd done it. He'd wanted to make me climax for him over and over. Once evidently hadn't been enough and I didn't mind one little bit.

With a shudder and a moan, he then joined me in the release and stilled. I tried to climb off him, but still wasn't able to move. I couldn't until Tommy put me down and let me untangle my legs so we simply stayed there while he composed himself.

When I was finally free, I grabbed some paper towels from the box on the dash just in time to catch the wetness trickling between my thighs. I'd always found it gross, but it was just one of those things I had learnt to tackle after a bit of fun in the sack. A lesson no one had needed to teach me about, but one I'd learned for myself when I'd become a woman and taken charge of my body during sex.

"Damn, woman. I thought we were meant to be going for a walk?" Tommy teased as he put himself away. I didn't answer, I just shrugged and offered him a salacious smile.

I was back in the passenger side and almost ready when he opened the driver's side door and jumped down and out of sight. Next thing I knew, Tommy had my door open and his hand stretched out for me to take.

I let him lift me down, like a gentleman, before groaning as I took in the trail ahead of us—if you could call it that. It was a proper mountain path with a steep incline. Not for the faint of heart.

"Tommy, I'm not cut out for a hike right now," I grumbled, but he took off anyway.

I figured I had two choices, wait in the truck, or follow him.

So I did the latter of course.

It was when I caught him up that I realized he had more than just a backpack full of snacks on his back. "Not just a walk planned I see," I said, indicating to the supplies on his shoulders. I could see roll mats and a small tent, so wasn't surprised when he told me we were spending the night beneath the stars.

I didn't mind though. Growing up a military kid, I'd done all sorts of wilderness training over the years, usually for fun but sometimes for sport. Before I'd left home and headed for the bright lights of LA I was one of the volunteers at the local school and would take the kids on bug hunts and nature walks over the summer or on weekends. I knew which berries were good and which mushrooms were even better. I knew how to start a fire from scratch and how best to tap water from a tree. Not that Tommy knew any of that, of course. He seemed to think he was teaching me a thing or two by having me come up the mountain alongside him and I was more than happy to let him carry on. He didn't have to know everything.

After a few hours' spent hiking, we reached the top of a truly scenic peak and that was where Tommy decided we would make our camp for the night. Personally, I would've chosen a spot closer to the tree line, but I was still letting him take charge so just sat back and let him do his thing while I sipped on some water and ate some trail mix he'd handed me.

Tommy made quick work of it and seemed to have finished setting up the tent and our beds, but then he reached into the pack and pulled out one more length of rope. I eyed it curiously as he tugged on it, testing the strength. "What's that for?" I asked.

"I'll show you after dinner," he replied, setting up a small gas stove for us to boil some food on. He was utterly at ease with nature and I knew he'd done this all a ton of times before.

I watched mesmerized as he then tore open some food packets and cooked us up a hearty stew. It reminded me of the ration packs my dad would bring home from work sometimes. Random meals all squished together but that still tasted amazing because we only ever ate them when we too had been hiking for hours or working hard on whatever project he had us involved in. I closed my eyes and the smell took me right back to my childhood.

"I like being here with you," I told him, forgetting where I was for a second, and whom I was with. I was in the company of either my tormentor or my protector, whichever one Tommy decided he wanted to be, so I knew I couldn't show any signs of weakness with him otherwise he'd pounce all over it I could tell.

"If you like it so much, perhaps you'll let me make our night a little more memorable?" he enquired and I couldn't deny being intrigued.

"How?" I asked as I cleaned up our dinner bowls and then packed them away. Tommy answered by getting up and walking over to the tent he'd made up for us to sleep in. He lifted the awning and beckoned me inside, so I wandered closer.

"Wait, no shoes," he demanded and I rolled my eyes but still kicked off my boots before clambering into the tent. It was small and cramped inside. Not enough room to stand in but our two roll mats and sleeping bags fit perfectly so was more than enough. "Take off your clothes," Tommy ordered, breaking my reverie. I did as he'd asked and was soon kneeling before him stark naked. He watched me for a few seconds and then went to the pack he'd stashed the rope away in.

I inhaled sharply. I didn't want to be tied up again and shook my head no, but Tommy reacted to my refusal by grabbing the back of my neck and forcing me down onto the pillow face first. And all with the biggest smile on his darkly handsome face.

I squealed and tried to fight him off me, but he was far too strong. It still didn't stop me from trying, though. The cushion muffled my screams and pleas but I still writhed and kicked, trying my hardest to get out of his hold.

It was no use. Tommy had my wrists bound in seconds and then tied them to my ankles before I could so much as register what he was doing. In my panic, I tried to twist and pull at the ropes in a bid to get free, and what made it worse was how I was unable to see or speak thanks to the pillow almost smothering me. It was torture and I couldn't stand it. And Tommy was clearly in tormentor mode because he was doing nothing but watch me squirm.

I forced myself to get a grip and turned my head to the side, where I breathed a sigh of relief when he brushed my hair out of my face, peering down at me.

"Please, Tommy. I don't like it," I begged. He shushed me and then ran his hands down my back, where he delivered a heavy-handed slap to one of my ass cheeks.

"I told you what I am. The things I want," he reminded me. "And you promised to deliver them, Piper. Don't let me down."

I didn't know how else I could play his game other

than beg for him to stop. He wanted to torment me and he was doing just that, so I let out an angry moan and fought against my binds again. And then it dawned on me. He needed something else. Not begging or bargaining, but something far more primal. Something more vulgar and cruel.

"It's not worth the hassle," I demanded, feeling angry and ready once again to let it show. "You're not worth it. I fucking hate you."

I saw the rage flash in Tommy's eyes and it felt good to elicit such a strong reaction from him. Two could play this game and I was going to make damn sure he knew I was no weak little girl for him to toy with.

SIXTEEN

Tommy

I had never wanted to hurt a woman as much as I wanted to hurt Piper in that moment. A voice in my head was screaming for me to teach her a proper lesson. To punch and kick her into submission. Then we'd see who was boss.

Instead, I left her there to stew on her words and made a sharp exit from the tent so I didn't have to look at her any longer. I was liable to slap more than just her backside if she didn't bite her fucking tongue.

I zipped the entryway closed, locking her inside, not that she could escape the binds, but I needed an extra barrier between us. She was calling out to me, saying she was sorry, but I could hardly hear her over the sound of the blood rushing through my skull.

My heart was pounding hard. My cock even harder. I ignored them both as I built up the fire and relit it, watching the sun as it began to creep lower on the horizon.

I was just about finished when I heard feet moving over the gravel on the trail above us. I could tell Piper had heard it too because she finally shut the hell up and I grinned to myself, thinking how terrified she must be of anyone finding her in such a predicament. I looked up and nodded, lifting my hand in greeting to the hikers on their way down the mountain, and then received two smile-and-wave gestures in return.

"Hey, are you Tommy Darke?" the first of the hikers then asked after he'd rounded the bend and reached the part of the trail we'd come off at. He was close enough to see me properly and seemed over the moon to have stumbled on a Hollywood A-lister in the mountains.

"Yeah, in the flesh," I replied and then grinned inwardly as he and his friend came off the trail towards me. God, Piper must be shitting herself in that tent listening to this, and I intended to make it ten times worse. "You heading back down?" I asked when they were closer and the guy nodded. "Come and sit with me. You've got time before sunset."

They looked like all their Christmas's had come at once and immediately dropped their packs before taking a seat on them so as to avoid the cold ground.

We caught up for a few minutes and the guys told me how they'd spent the previous two days scaling San Gabriel's peaks. They were evidently keen hikers and I liked their style. In fact, I quite liked the pair of them in general. They were fun to talk to and seemed adventurous. Just like me.

Even though we were chatting away, my eyes kept darting to the tent and I was imagining Piper inside cursing my name while trying her hardest not to make a sound. I wanted to push her further. Make her hate me just that little bit more. "Oh, hey. You wanna see something cool?" I asked before letting them go finish their hike.

"Yeah, sure," the first one said and they watched me as I went over to the tent and began unzipping the door just enough so that I could poke my head inside.

There she was, my little captive. Piper looked beyond

terrified. Just as I'd hoped. But of course, she was out of sight to the others. Only I could see her gorgeous face and stunning nakedness. After all, it didn't matter that I wanted to push her, she was mine to torment and enjoy. Not theirs. It was all I could do to hide my smile though as I reached inside and grabbed my cell before closing the zipper again.

I then proceeded to show the guys some snaps from the latest movie on my phone before taking a selfie I promised I would upload the second I was back in cell reception range. The two guys were over the moon and thanked me profusely, which sure caressed my ego nicely. They could come around more often. No, on second thoughts I'd rather be alone with my girl and decided it was time they left. I wrapped things up and we said our goodbyes before I sat by the fire and watched the tops of their heads disappear down the mountain. I also listened to be sure they'd definitely gone before clambering back into the tent and began pulling Piper free from her binds.

She freaked when I'd untied her. I could understand it, but damn, she was hot when she was angry. I let her hit me a few times and spew curses my way, and then I'd had enough. It was time I dished out just a little bit more brutality. Or maybe a lot. I wasn't sure when I'd stop, only that at some point I'd flip that switch and all would be well.

I grabbed Piper by the throat and pushed her facedown onto the pillow again, unbuttoning my fly with my free hand as I did so. I then pushed my pants down my thighs and knees, eventually kicking them off into a heap at the end of the tent. Piper still resisted me and I answered by pressing her face harder into the cushion. She went limp when I forced open her knees with mine, but it didn't matter that she'd finally stopped fighting me. I was taking what was mine and nothing was going to stop me.

Piper was soaking wet and I slid right inside without any need to coat myself in her juices for lubrication first. I almost came then and there.

"Were you ready for me, Piper," I groaned as I began pushing in and out. "You feel ready."

"Fuck you," she croaked in response and I laughed loudly as I did just that. I pounded into her and Piper pushed back against me, her pussy clenching around my cock as I burrowed deeper and deeper into her. "Stop, Tommy," she then begged. "Please. I think I'm gonna pee!"

I didn't stop. Something about the entire scenario made me want it darker and more depraved. I wanted Piper to piss herself while I continued to hold her down and fuck her. I wanted to see the humiliation such an act would bring.

She came and her writhing and clenching was enough to drive me over the edge so I joined her in the climax and then peered down at the sleeping bag beneath her. Damn it, she'd managed to hold her bladder and I was uncannily disappointed.

As soon as I let her go, Piper threw on her shirt and flew outside into the darkness of the night. I yanked on my boxers and a jacket and followed her into the bushes where I watched as she took a piss. The longest piss in the world, without a doubt. It went on forever but I was enthralled as I watched her let go. Mesmerized by the relief on her face as she crouched there soaking the bushes beneath that fine behind of hers.

When it was over, I saw her do a little shake and began to laugh. Piper looked so silly it was endearing, so I went to the tent and grabbed a roll of toilet paper I'd brought along for us to use. I then wrapped some around my palm, looping it over and over before ripping it along the perforated edge. She seemed surprised when I met her halfway between the tent and her designated toilet area and shoved my wrapped up hand between her thighs to soak up any remains of her piss. "Don't, that's dirty," she squealed, trying to pull away, but I wouldn't let her. I felt the few droplets of pee left on her dirty cunt soak into the tissue and grinned. I liked it dirty.

My tastes for her were getting darker by the minute, I could tell, but I also didn't care. I just hoped she was ready, because something inside of me seemed to sense we were only just getting started.

SEVENTEEN

Piper

After I was nicely dried up thanks to Tommy's weird way of helping me, I dragged the tissue paper over his knuckles and threw in our makeshift trash bag over by the tent before soaking both our palms in alcohol rub.

He certainly was an oddball, I'd give him that, and an infuriating ass for sure. But there was still so much that excited me about him. Something that made me want to push his buttons regardless of knowing there was no remorse when it came to him retaliating if he was in one of his torturous moods. I was playing with fire and, even though I knew it was foolish, I wasn't afraid to get burned.

I grabbed my pants from the tent and slid my legs inside, already feeling the chill leeching into my skin and bones now that night had fallen. And then I climbed back into my boots and jacket. Tommy did the same and I watched as he stoked the fire back to life and threw a few pieces of wood onto it to revive the flames. It wasn't long at all until it was blazing nicely and he sat down, beckoning me over with a soft smile. I went to him hesitantly. I had to know what I was getting myself into by approaching him and I think he knew.

"Come here. Let me care for you, Piper," he told me.

I shook my head no. There was no way I could go for another round in the sack. I was beyond sore between my legs and felt exhausted and achy all over after having been tied up for the better part of an hour. Tommy held my gaze, his hand still outstretched in summoning. "I know what you need. Let me give it to you. Trust me…"

Did I trust him? I thought so, but then why was I hesitating? I think I needed to be sure that he'd flipped his switch, but Tommy was giving nothing more away. Against all my instincts telling me not to go to him, I went weak at the knees. His face was so gentle and calm. His tone of voice seemed sincere and I ignored all of my better judgments telling me not to trust him. I put my faith in the man who had just moments before held me against my will and then fucked me while pinning me down by my throat. *Not like you didn't love it,* I reminded myself.

I went to Tommy and fell into his lap when he yanked me down, which seemed exactly where he wanted me. He then cradled me and wrapped his arms around my body so tightly I very quickly forgot all about the cold. All I could see was the concave at the base of his neck, and my forehead was tucked against his cheek. All I could smell was his heady musk and I breathed it in with relish.

I was besotted with this dark and dangerous creature and knew it. No matter what he'd done, our moments like this made it all worth it and I basked in his strong arms, expecting him to pull away again any moment, but he didn't. Tommy continued to hold me pressed tightly against him for what felt like hours.

He shushed me whenever I tried to ask him what was going on. All he let be said between us were words of adoration and love. He made me feel wanted and cared for again. Not remotely like a plaything he enjoyed tormenting or a quickie bit of fun. I felt like his one true love and knew I loved him in return, and all while neither of us spoke more than a few words.

Then and there, realization struck.

I was Tommy's girl now and there was no going back.

Not that I wanted to.

After breakfast the next morning, we packed up the tent and started the walk back down to where Tommy had parked the truck. It didn't take us long, and while I didn't fret over it, part of me wondered what we would do if we came across any other hikers like Tommy had the evening before. Would we make some lame attempt at explaining why we were walking together in the woods? Would anyone even care? I didn't know, but part of me was intrigued to find out. I wanted to see what Tommy said and did if it happened. Whether he would put an arm around me and tell them I was his girl or if he'd play it cool and dumb down our relationship by telling whoever it was that we were just friends.

I didn't get my answer because we reached the truck without seeing another soul and I climbed up into the passenger side with a sigh. I wanted to come right out and ask him if he'd considered it, but Tommy seemed so relaxed I didn't want to ruin the mood by making him have 'the talk' with me. I managed to convince myself that I wasn't one of those girls and wasn't going to cave just because I was having a girlie moment and forced it all away.

We reached the cabin after a short and quiet drive and I was beyond glad to see the huge wooden building ahead of us. I needed to shower badly.

We headed inside and I helped Tommy unload the kit before hitting the bathroom. There, I locked the door and undressed before turning on the jets of the large shower.

I also checked myself over in the mirror and, true to Tommy's word, I didn't have a bruise or a scratch on me. In spite of everything we'd been doing together and how aggressive his dark side seemed, no one who looked at me would be any the wiser. My clever lover knew his stuff.

As I climbed into the warm cascade from the showerheads above, I was reminded of my old life. One where I was timid and downtrodden. Where I had a man whom I adored but who never took care of me the way Tommy did, and I felt a lump form in my throat just thinking back to those days. I knew I couldn't pour my heart out to Tommy because I could never talk about Damon without breaking down and letting my tears flow, and that was the one rule he'd insisted upon. I was never allowed to cry in front of Tommy. For whatever reason, they were a trigger for him, and one I didn't want to have to test the theory on. I'd take his word for it, thank you very much.

And so, I cried into my hands, letting the water wash my tears down the plughole and out of sight. I felt lucky to have Tommy and happy that he loved me, but also terrified of losing him. I couldn't imagine ever wanting this thing between us to end and even the thought of it broke my heart in two, making the tears flow harder.

Man, I was in serious trouble.

EIGHTEEN

Tommy

Piper was taking so long in the bathroom that I found myself growing more and more annoyed. What was she playing at? We had one more night together before we both had to head back to the city for work and she was wasting time primping and preening? I had a quick shower in the en-suite and as the hot water cleansed away the grime of our busy trip to the mountain, a thought crept into my mind. I wanted her at my mercy again, but this time, I was going to do it differently. No manhandling involved, just some good old manipulation.

I shut off the water and dried quickly so I could get started on the plan forming in my mind. The first step was simple. All I had to do was get her drunk. Out in the kitchen, I poured her a glass of wine and made myself a whiskey and soda using the teensiest bit of liquor. Just enough so she'd be able to smell it on me and taste it on my lips.

When Piper finally emerged from the bathroom, I plucked the glass by its stem and offered it to her with a dashing smile, reveling in the flush that instantly flooded her cheeks as she regarded me. My girl certainly was smitten. In all fairness, she enamored me, too. All she had to do was bat those lashes of hers and I wanted to bury myself so deeply inside of her she'd feel it in her navel. I wanted to be with her always and keep watch over her, day and night. I knew this now.

She wasn't free of me and I hoped she accepted the truth of it by now—that she never would be.

I plied Piper with drink after drink while I had little more than a couple shots' worth of whiskey. I pretended to get drunk alongside her while we sat and chatted together and I listened as she told me about her life before she'd moved to Los Angeles—as if I hadn't already done plenty of homework on her and knew exactly what army bases she'd lived in and when. Such a fool she was to let herself fall for the monster, but she loved it, I could tell.

I played along, but all the while I dominated her and everything around her. Using my body language, I made a point of physically overshadowing Piper, and before long she was showing signs of natural submission. She began mirroring my gestures and movements, even my facial expressions. When I took a sip of my drink, so did she, and when I smiled or frowned, I noticed she did too.

I went one step further and instructed that she sit on my lap, and then didn't give her the option of moving into any other position than strewn across me. Only when she was in need of a top up did I move, but even then, she came along to the bar with me.

I had to keep her in my hands. To feel her, and Piper was beyond complaint. She followed me and my black heart no matter where I went.

It wasn't long before my tiny love was blind drunk and I decided to put on some music so I could hold her even closer. I decided on a slow, melodic track and pulled Piper to me, wrapping my arms around her shoulders.

A smile played on my lips as she slipped her hands around my waist and I grinned back. So, she was still sober enough to know what she was doing. I wanted to rectify that. I wondered if perhaps next time I should pick up some sleeping pills to crush and put in her wine as well. That ought to do the trick in making her my slave. Mine to do with as I pleased, like a living doll.

The image of her glassy-eyed and out of it entered my head and I grimaced. No. I didn't want that. I wanted Piper laid back with her legs open and her taking every inch of me while screaming, begging for more. Drunk and compliant would do nicely.

"You love me, don't you?" I whispered and Piper hummed in response. That wasn't good enough. I pulled back from our embrace and peered down at her darkly. "You love me, don't you?" I asked again. Piper's eyes rolled up to look into my face and she swayed thanks to the copious amounts of booze in her system.

"Yes. I love you, Tommy," she croaked.

"Why?" I demanded, suddenly needing to know.

She thought about it for a moment and then grinned. Her face lit up like the goddamn Fourth of July and she giggled.

"Because you're weird, Tommy. You're so frickin' fucked up but I love it, and I guess that makes me weird, too."

I had to laugh. She sure was right.

NINETEEN

Piper

I woke the next day feeling like death. I didn't know if I wanted to get up and hurl or just lie there a little longer and pray I kept my shit together. I sure didn't want Tommy to see me puke. God, how much had I had to drink? He'd kept up with my pace though so I figured he had to be feeling as bad as me, but that didn't make me any better.

A shiver swept over me and I finally opened my eyes to discover I was naked and had kicked off the bed sheets. Tommy wasn't there so I quickly clambered to my feet and was just pulling on a shirt when he appeared in the doorway.

How could he look so damn good? I wanted to throttle him.

"Morning beautiful," he chimed and then handed me a smoothie. "Drink this, it'll do you wonders." I did as he said while he watched me curiously as though he were scrutinizing a piece of art or something.

"How much did we drink last night?" I asked once my glass was empty.

"A lot," he laughed before turning and heading back out the way he'd come in. I watched him go, not having the energy to move too much, but had to admit it felt good to have some food in my stomach.

Once I was feeling a little more human I followed Tommy out into the lounge, hoping my hangover might not be so bad after all thanks to his wonder-smoothie.

"I'm sorry if I was a mess," I said when I reached him. There weren't many blank spots in my memory, but I did remember chewing his ear off for a while about my issues with my parents and how hard some of the fresh starts had been. I didn't think I'd said anything about Damon and wasn't sure I ever could, at least not with Tommy. In many ways they were so alike, but at least Tommy treated me with kindness. At least he cared. Not like Damon who had left me a shell of a woman by the time I'd finally had enough of his ways and broken free.

There were things I then suddenly remembered clearly from my drunken night the evening before. Moments such as him holding me close and telling me I was his. As if I'd needed reminding? I knew it in every inch of my heart and soul, regardless of what I'd tried to tell myself about being a strong and independent woman who didn't need a man in her life to know it was worthwhile. No need for validation. Yeah, who was I kidding? I needed all of those things just like any other young woman and luckily for me, Tommy was giving me everything and then some.

He regarded me, watching as my emotions changed from up to down and back again in a heartbeat.

"You weren't a mess last night at all, Piper," he told me sternly. "Don't ever say sorry to me."

My breath hitched in my throat. How could he say such a thing? I began to doubt everything I'd thought I knew about our relationship simply because it felt too good to be true. Was he lying to me? Was I a fool for believing that this could work when we both knew there was darkness in him that demanded he torture me when it called to him?

One that I had called forth from the depths of his soul and was forced to take responsibility for now that it'd come to the surface.

I had somehow come to accept how I needed to care for that dark side of his. To nurture it. Fool or not, I wasn't going to walk away and we both knew it.

"Okay," I hummed and got the shock of my life when he crossed the room and pinned me to the wall behind.

Tommy gripped me by the throat and I was reminded once again of his volatile tendencies that were mine alone to bear the brunt of. No matter my acceptance of it, I was still terrified at seeing the rage in his eyes and felt myself wilt under the pressure.

"Do you need me to teach you a lesson about just what you're worth to me?"

"No," I croaked, but he didn't hear me. Tommy was lost to his dark whims and he dragged me toward the wooden deck without a care for how much I struggled against him. I was petrified of going out there and I realized he knew it. Evidently it truly was time I was properly punished. Tortured.

I knew what was coming before he'd even opened the door and thrown me out onto the damp wooden deck with a heartless thud.

He then slammed the door closed and clicked the lock, while all I could do was scream and beg for him to let me back inside, but I knew it was no use. I wouldn't be allowed back in until he said so, or at least not until he was finished with yet another of his awful games.

TWENTY

Tommy

This was it. The defining moment in my quest to have outright control over my darling Piper. I locked that door and lifted my arms above my head, leaning against the doorframe so I could watch her out the window, like the highest definition screen in the whole damn world.

She was hugging the outside of the door while screaming in pure terror, pressing her ass against the glass in a bid to stay as close to the actual house as possible. I was captivated. This wasn't my doing but her fear of heights and I loved seeing her fall apart. Part of me wanted to break her even more. To remove every shackle she had holding her down and leave her with only me. Perhaps save her, or better yet, torment her even more?

I could hear Piper sucking in hitched breaths and my cock hardened at the sound. When she then slumped to the floor and curled into a ball like some wounded creature trying to protect itself, I let myself smile for a moment before booting the door to get her attention.

Piper looked up at me with venom in her eyes. She was beyond furious with me and that was fine by me. All part of my new favorite game.

"Walk to the end of the balcony and back, then I'll let you back in…" I told her.

She looked to the edge of the deck and then back at me, shaking her head frantically.

"I can't, Tommy. Please just let me back in," she begged. I didn't answer. I simply continued to watch her process her options. If she did it, she'd be back inside and in my arms within minutes. Then I'd flip my switch and care for her. Make it all better again. I might even make love to her again. That was nice.

But first, she had to do this one little thing. Sadly for her, it was the one thing she was terrified of doing. I couldn't understand why though. The deck was perfectly safe and it annoyed the hell out of me that she had left herself believe otherwise. To not trust me and listen to her irrational brain instead.

She eventually stood and I could see her calming her frantic breaths. I could then hear her talking to herself, urging her feet to move forward, and before long she took a tentative step onto the next plank. I could see her trembling violently and knew it had nothing to do with the cold. It was actually rather mild out there, so I knew her shivers had more to do with her fear than any morning chill.

Well, at least she'd forgotten all about her hangover.

It felt like an age, but eventually Piper moved forward onto the next board, and the next. She made it to the end, touched the ledge, and hotfooted it back over to the doorway, which I'd unlocked and had open at the ready for her.

TWENTY-ONE

Piper

I ran through that doorway and straight past Tommy without even looking at him. I didn't feel elated for having conquered one of my fears. No way. I was still terrified of that deck, perhaps even more so now, and hated that it was him who had put me out on there to begin with. This wasn't fun anymore and I wanted out.

I ran to the bedroom and grabbed my things, stuffing them back in my suitcase without any care for crumpling my nice clothes or whether my perfume leaked all over the place. I just needed to get out of there.

It didn't matter the promises I'd made both Tommy and myself about letting him torture me. He'd gone too far this time. I'd almost had a panic attack out there and it was far from fun or exciting. It was downright petrifying. Thank God for my years of therapy and my ability to talk myself down now that I'd learned the best ways to overcome my heightened anxiety.

I felt ruined. Broken. This wasn't fun.

I was leaving.

Tommy tried to reason with me and he also tried to

hold me, evidently ready to flip his internal switch, but I wasn't ready to listen or to calm down. I needed some air. Some space.

I grabbed my keys and headed for the door. Outside, I threw myself and my things in my car and pressed the button that ought to have switched the engine on. Nothing happened. I let out a loud roar in fury.

"Asshole!" I screamed, looking up to find Tommy watching me from the doorway with a smile. I wasn't going to give him the satisfaction of watching me walk back inside. Back to him. Instead, I climbed out and slammed my car door closed before I started walking back towards the main road that I'd driven up the mountain via. I'd hitchhike home if I had to. Anything was better than staying there with him.

I tried not to look back. Not to check if he was following me, but I couldn't help myself. Right before I turned a bend that I knew would leave me without sight of his cabin, I looked back over my shoulder and found Tommy continuing to watch me from the doorway. Still half-dressed and as calm as ever, he simply watched me walk away as though so sure I'd only get so far before turning back. I flipped him the bird and kept on going. All I wanted was to get home.

I talked to myself as I pounded the pavement. Calling myself an idiot and cursing Tommy and everything he meant to me.

Just as I was coming up to the main road, I heard a twig snap somewhere in the trees to my right and came to a stop. Was he there? No, he couldn't be. It had to be an animal or something. Tommy would've just come down the path if he wanted to chase after me, surely?

I kept on walking.

I could see some cars driving past the turnoff and picked up speed. I'd flag one down and say I'd broken down after a hike up the mountain. No one would need to know I'd been there with Tommy. Our secrets would remain just that.

Right before I reached the road, I heard another twig snap but this time I ignored it. I immediately wished I hadn't.

Thick, strong arms enveloped me from behind and lifted me off the ground. I screamed and my attacker put a hand over my mouth. I knew it was Tommy but that didn't stop me from writhing and trying to break out of his hold. The last thing I wanted was to go back to that cabin. I wasn't ready for him to tell me he was sorry and try to make it up to me. No sir. He needed to pay first. To beg me for forgiveness.

I jabbed him with my elbows and tried to kick, but it was no use. Tommy dragged me into the bushes and flung me against a tree, pressing into me from behind.

"You shouldn't have run from me, Piper," he groaned in my ear before releasing my mouth.

"I didn't run. I stormed away because you're an asshole who didn't deserve for me to stay."

He turned me to face him and I thought for a minute he might slap me. He looked ready to strike, as if I'd hit a nerve.

"You need to let me take care of you," he said, but his eyes were still dark. I didn't trust that he'd flipped his switch and was going to be soft and kind. Plus, I was still too angry to want it. "I have to do both otherwise it won't work." He unbuttoned my pants and I pushed him away.

"No," I demanded. "Not here and not like this. It isn't love if I'm still hurting."

Tommy grabbed my hands and held them in one of his, still going for my pants with his free hand.

"Let me show you, Piper. It'll feel better after I make you see how much I love you," he pleaded, but I was having none of it. Tommy had gone too far this time and he couldn't make up for it by fucking me.

"This isn't love," I repeated, but he carried on. He pulled my pants down a little and panic started to rise in my chest. I didn't want it. Not there. Not like that. The games were over but Tommy was going to take something I didn't want to give him and that wasn't going to be okay with me.

I felt my eyes well up in fear and I knew what to do. What would make him back off and leave me be. I let the tears fall. The moment he saw them, Tommy paled. He looked like I'd just torn his heart out and stomped on it, and he immediately backed off. I hated it, but was also glad I had been able to stop him before things had taken a direction we'd both have regretted.

Once I was free, I pulled my pants back up and buttoned them before I then stumbled away, heading for the road again.

"Wait," Tommy pleaded, and I was about to tell him to go to hell when I turned back and saw the agony in his eyes, but also the iciness. Like I had broken him, too. Good. "Take my truck," was all he added, throwing me the keys. I caught them and nodded, but didn't thank him. There was no need given how he was clearly responsible for my own car being dead.

I turned and walked away, hiding the fresh tears streaming down my face. They had already served their purpose and I didn't feel the need to torture Tommy further by showing him them any more.

My heart felt like it was breaking with every step away from him I took. The moment was far from anything I'd hoped for when I'd awoken that morning and I knew it'd haunt me until the end of my days.

His aggressive touch. That violent, tortured face. Gone had been my gorgeous and cock-sure lover, and I had crumbled. The walk back up towards the cabin was a hard one. I felt slow and exhausted. As if our altercation had completely taken it out of me. When I reached the two cars parked side-by-side in front of the cabin, I was glad to be leaving it all behind me.

I grabbed my things and jumped in the driver's side,

and then I drove away without so much as looking for Tommy on the road back down. I drove like my life depended on it and reached home in record time.

I even left his car on my driveway, not caring who might recognize it, and ran inside, double-locking the doors behind me. Without checking my mail or listening to my voice messages, I went straight up to my room where I showered and then climbed into bed. That's where I stayed for the twenty or so hours that followed. My phone rang a few times and I could hear Janie's angry voice on the machine as she left me messages demanding to know where I was and if I was okay. But I wasn't okay, and I wasn't sure I ever would be. I couldn't face telling her or anyone else what'd happened, so I hid away. Locked the doors, closed the drapes and blocked out the world.

My plan worked fine until I got an email directly from the PR team for *Wayward* outlining the press dates and commitments I was expected to attend. Janie had given up calling and I soon knew why when she was banging down my door, so I flung it open and glared at her.

"I know, okay!" I demanded.

"No, it's not okay," she replied angrily. "Where the fuck have you been, Piper? You said a few days and it's been over a week. I was worried."

I looked past Janie to my driveway where I expected Tommy's truck to still be parked. I was surprised she hadn't asked me about it and got my answer when I saw my little soft top nestled in its usual spot beneath my tree. Tommy had brought it back and taken his truck away. When had he done it? Had he tried snooping in my windows to see what I was up to while he was here? If he had it wouldn't have been a pretty sight I knew that much. I'd hardly taken care of myself other than showering and scraping my hair back while either crying myself to sleep or eating everything I could get my hands on while watching TV. Yeah, super sexy.

"I've had a hard few days, that's all," I told Janie, who was still staring at me with what appeared to be genuine concern in her eyes. "I… I kinda broke up with someone I thought meant something to me," I revealed and Janie sighed in what I presumed was relief that I wasn't having some random meltdown.

I turned and went back inside but left the door open in welcome for her to follow me, which of course she did.

"We've all been there, babe," she said as she took a seat beside me on the sofa and took a look around at my empty home. One thing I wasn't was a slob, so luckily my house wasn't in a state, but I still hated her seeing me like this, even if it was nice to have a shoulder to cry on. "Whoever he is, he's a damn fool to have lost you. What you need is to focus on work. Drive yourself forward rather than back and don't let anyone or anything bring you down."

I had to stifle fresh tears. Janie had given me that same talk a few years before and I nodded. She was right, like always.

"What do you have in mind?" I asked with a smile, and was glad she hadn't asked for more details regarding the source of my heartbreak. One thing Janie had going for her was she wasn't one to pry. She was no doubt dying to know who had broken my heart but she wouldn't come right out and say it. If I offered up the details she wouldn't refuse to hear the ins and outs, don't get me wrong, but she was a kind enough soul to see I was hurting and she wanted to help take my mind off the situation at hand.

"Well, if you'd just answered your goddam phone!" she teased before handing me her tablet. Open on it was a set of photographs that took my breath away. It was all I could do not to start crying again, but I forced the tears away. I focused on rebuilding my walls rather than let them come crashing down again.

The pictures were the promo shots Tommy and I had taken together the few days previously. They were incredible. More than that, they were the perfect portrayal of heat and tension between two people.

George and Penny.

Tommy and Piper.

Two actors and their chemistry caught on camera for all to see. God, he was beautiful. I felt a pang of yearning hit me for the first time since I'd come flying through that patio door from the deck of the cabin. I didn't want to feel those things for him. To want him. And yet there I was, staring at his photograph like a lovesick teenager…

"These are amazing," I eventually whispered as I handed the device back to Janie.

"No shit," she replied with a wide smile. "They're going public during your interview with Tommy and Scarlet on the *Nightly Show* this weekend."

I wanted to feel excited or nervous about being live on television in front of millions of viewers, when instead I was still numb. I was desperate to care that the movie was getting some decent exposure and so too would I. To hope people would be excited to see it. I wanted to care about anything other than missing him, but all I could think of was that horrible yet remarkable man and how I wished he hadn't ruined things.

"Let's celebrate," I told Janie as I jumped up off the sofa and grabbed her hand. "I feel like going to a crazily expensive and exclusive club and dancing to music by bands I can't even pronounce the names of while I get shitfaced. What do you say?"

"Well… if one of my jobs as your ever-loyal manager isn't to keep you out of trouble on drunken nights out, I don't know what is," she replied with a grin, but I wasn't buying it. She wasn't just my manager, but my friend too. I had known that for a long time and I also knew they were very hard to come by nowadays. I was going to make sure she knew I appreciated the hell out of her for turning up at my house and forcing me out of my funk, and was going to start by taking her out and endeavoring to have the night of our lives.

TWENTY-TWO

Tommy

When had I last slept? I wasn't actually sure. But sleep was overrated and unnecessary anyway. Especially when I had an obsession that'd seemed to override every other need.

I'd been sneaking around for days and was glad I'd been keeping abreast of her movements when I saw Piper and her friend walk out of her house both dressed up like whores. I followed them and pulled my truck to a stop while I watched the pair climb out of the limo they'd hired and head straight toward the doorman at one of LA's most prestigious nightclubs. The guy took one look at her and plucked that rope he was the king of to let her pass, much to the distaste of some of the people queuing to get in. But she deserved that kind of treatment. Piper had earned it. This town knew her name and showed her some respect, and all while I was utterly consumed by her. That damn woman had wormed her way inside my skin and then ripped her way back out again without a care for the carnage she'd left behind. I'd seen her tears and backed off, but it'd been more than that. Piper had broken me. I had puked my guts up in the bushes the minute she'd gone. I'd felt repulsed by the mere suggestion of her let alone the sight of her, and had been glad when my truck had torn down the long drive and out of sight.

I'd then gone back to the cabin and taken a chainsaw to that deck. The hot tub was now in pieces and the wooden boards carved up and thrown down onto the mountainside below. But I had still felt the same. Nothing had made me feel better. Not drinking myself into a stupor or watching violent pornography and even snuff films while jerking off so hard I gave myself friction burns. The only thing that'd helped was watching *her.*

Sneaking glimpses from the shadows after I'd let myself in with my secret key while she'd slept.

Spying on her from the garden when she passed the cracks in her curtains during the day.

My poor Piper had looked like shit, and rightly so. I would've bet I looked like shit, too.

I toyed with the idea of going inside the club so I could watch her, but decided against it. Someone was bound to recognize me or tip off the paparazzi and I didn't want her to find out about me being so hot on her tail. Following her around like some lovesick puppy.

That wasn't what I was doing it for, though. I was doing it because Piper was mine. She belonged to me and had tried to get away, but I wasn't going to allow it. Didn't she know by now that she'd never escape me?

She deserved to be punished and I wanted to find the best way to do it. But first, I'd known I had to do the reconnaissance work. To figure out her next steps by knowing Piper inside and out. Not only that, but also by making her do what I wanted. By manipulating her. Controlling every aspect of her life so she had no one but me. And then I would be there with open arms, ready and raring to pick up the pieces.

I would've been content to sit and wait for her out the front of the club, but then I noticed a group of guys being let inside ahead of the queue by the burly bouncer. I recognized the one at the head of them right away and felt my lips curl back from my teeth in a snarl.

Bradley Fucking Thomas.

I knew all about his history with Piper and how she'd been the one to put a stop to their liaisons rather than him. He was still interested. Of course he was, and my mind began to race with scenarios in which they rekindled that flame beneath the strobe lights of the club.

She was in there and still hated me, and seeing Bradley might just make her want to do something to hurt me. Something I would make it my mission to make her regret. She belonged to me and it didn't matter that she'd run away, I was happy to have to remind her of it sooner than later.

I drove back towards home and dialed up a few of my buddies on the way. They were more than happy to come and meet me for a night out at the club and I had to smile to myself as I got dressed. I pulled on a tight shirt that practically creaked when I flexed my biceps and a pair of pants I knew I looked hot in. Two could play this game of cat and mouse and I knew I would be the winner. I always was.

After looking at my reflection in the mirror for a few seconds I decided I was good to go. Ready for Piper to fall at my feet and beg for forgiveness. More than ready for the paparazzi and the screaming fans to come and gawk in awe of me. For them to clamber over themselves to have a mere glimpse of me. The one and only Tommy Darke.

I didn't mean to be bigheaded, but I knew I'd get plenty of attention once I got to the club and not just because of my epic stardom. I mean, I looked great, who wouldn't want to come and fawn all over me? Gone was the scrawny young man I'd once been and in his place was a toned and sculpted Adonis—if I did say so myself. I'd worked hard to develop the body I now had and it hadn't come easy. The same was easily said for my good looks I'd had to endure a lot to attain. A secret nose job and an operation to bring forward what was once a weak jaw had left me with perfectly asymmetrical features, which was apparently what almost all women found attractive in a lover and had certainly gotten me my share of tail. The years of having fixed braces had then fixed my crooked teeth and of course there were the hours I spent at the barbers having my hair trimmed to perfection along with my designer stubble to thank for the rest.

Yep, I was a Hollywood boy through and through. I was one of them now. I did the work and was vain enough to dedicate every waking moment I had to my biggest asset—me. I had been accepted into the fold and I knew I could never leave. No part of me even wanted to.

I closed my eyes and imagined Piper. What was she doing? Probably drinking too much and dancing with that friend of hers I'd seen her go in with. Maybe they were talking about boys and Piper was telling her about me. About how she loved it when I'd stalked her and had sneaked into her home to fuck her.

Damn, now I was rocking a huge hard on just imagining those cheeks of hers flushing while she told her friend about our exploits. I grabbed my cell and pulled up one of my new favorite porn websites. One that catered to the ever so darker tastes. Within seconds I'd found the recording I was after and I watched as the girl on the screen was tied up and humiliated by the man fucking her raw.

I was going to re-create this scene with Piper as her punishment for running away from me at the cabin. I unzipped my fly, gripped my cock, and began grinding into my hand. It was no time at all before I'd come into the tissue I'd plucked from the nearby box and I let out a deep sigh.

Piper wasn't going to know what hit her when I got my ruthless hands on her again.

I got back to the club and found my friends waiting for me in the queue. The look on their faces told me they'd tried their luck with the doorman and had been told to get in line like everyone else. They were basically nobodies, so I couldn't understand why they'd even tried without me, but I hid my disdain. They were my cover and I wanted to keep them sweet. But still, I didn't pluck them from the line. Instead I just lifted my finger telling them to wait. I'd handle it.

The doorman, Tony, and I went way back. He clapped me on the shoulder and grinned from ear to ear when I greeted him, as if he was surprised I'd remembered his name. We had a little bit of back and forth before I made it clear I wanted inside. The girls waiting nearby were calling my name, begging me to take them in with me and while I smiled and told them they looked lovely, I didn't offer any of them a place at my side. They were starstruck whores and I wasn't buying. Not tonight.

"Have you met my buddy Steve?" I asked Tony, who shook his head. I stepped back and hollered down the queue of people and right on cue, my three buddies jumped out of the line and came toward us. "He's just started work on a remake of that old western movie you love…"

That was all Tony needed to hear. He ushered me and the other two guys inside and promised to send Steve in after he'd gotten the scoop on the movie he told me he'd grown up watching as a kid. I didn't mind ditching Steve if it got us inside quicker. I could've gone in alone but I hated going in alone so the two guys I considered more acquaintances than friends would do for when I made my entrance.

I walked in first and was greeted by a set of doors I knew all too well. This club had been a favorite of mine before I'd delved deeper into the craft of method acting. Before, I would've been there every week, but now my work took precedence. I immersed myself in whatever my upcoming role dictated, but not tonight. Tonight I was just Tommy. Out on the town like old times.

The doors opened and I was hit by a wall of sound and pure bass. There were strobe lights and lasers that lit the place up and I soaked up the energy as we joined the sea of writhing bodies.

It thankfully didn't take long for me to lose the two hanger-on's. One look at the talent propping up the bar and they'd sidled away ready to try out their best pick-up lines, and while I'd promised to join them after saying hello to a few people, I had no intention of finding my way back to them. They'd served their purpose.

I spotted Bradley right away and made a beeline for him. So far, it appeared Piper was nowhere to be found, but at least she wasn't hanging off him so for the time being I was happy.

"Hey, Tommy," Bradley greeted me and I had to admit, he seemed more pleased to see me than I would've thought. It wasn't like we'd struck up a friendship while on set or anything.

I took a seat beside him and forced myself to smile.

"Hey," I replied coolly. "How's it goin'?"

"Good. Listen…" Brad said, suddenly looking sheepish. I frowned at him, wondering what he might be about to say. He stayed silent so I ordered a round of shots from the barmaid and did nothing more than watch him patiently. Enjoying watching him squirm. "Well, I guess I usually make more of an effort to get to know the people I'm working with so wanted to apologize for not inviting you out for a beer or anything after filming. I didn't feel like I was working with the real you, if you know what I mean?"

The barmaid returned with our drinks and I downed one. My first of the night. It burned that sweet, sweet heat in the back of my throat and I immediately took another. I watched Brad, feeling nothing but contempt for him.

Why would he think I'd want to go and have a beer

with him? We weren't friends and would never be. And he was wrong about one thing. He hadn't been working with me. He'd been working *for* me. Brad was my underling. My supporting actor. Nothing more.

"Say no more," I told him as I reached for another shot. "And don't feel bad, man. I'm here with my friends, I just wanted to come and say hi. You're right, it's not the same working with me on a movie because I'm not the same guy when I'm on set. I was George and he hated everyone." Brad laughed it off and shook his head as if he couldn't even begin to fathom what I was getting at.

I wanted to throttle him. To punch that grin off his smug face. I opened my mouth, ready to tell him to get back in his fucking box, but then stopped myself just in time. It wasn't me thinking that. It was George.

I was about to shut up and run. To avoid my inner mobster who seemed intent on making his comeback. But instead, I pushed those urges down. George was gone. I'd detoxed from him thanks to Piper so why the hell was he rearing his head now?

Brad didn't even seem to notice. He was peering over my shoulder and I saw as his eyes flashed with lust.

"Working with that one wasn't a chore though, was it?" he asked and I knew before I even turned to follow his line of sight who would be standing not far behind me.

Piper.

My Piper.

She was resplendent. A ray of goddam sunshine in my black world. She hadn't even seen me yet and still, I was burning with desire. I had to see her. To talk to her. Touch her. To fuck her. Discipline her…

When she finally saw me, I saw Piper's jaw clench and her eye flash with rage. Yes. That was what I was hoping for. I was still under her skin but she just didn't want to show it in front of Brad. *Make me punish you, Piper,* I thought. *Make me have to hurt you. Break you. Own you…*

She sauntered forward with a cunning smile curling at

her lips. She had a game to play with me, I could tell, so I let her come. Let her believe she had some control, when in fact, she had none.

I was going to make sure she knew it without any shadow of doubt before sunrise the following day.

"Well, if it isn't two of the hottest men I've had the privilege of working with," she whispered when she'd reached us, her voice low and husky. I then watched in awe as Piper licked her lips and came closer.

I didn't care who was in this club or who might be watching. I reacted to her presence. I stood taller and more commanding, dominating her and everyone else in this room. Or at least that was how I felt. Like a god. Someone she should worship and adore. One she should obey.

TWENTY-THREE

Piper

I should've run the moment I'd spotted him. I knew that. But I couldn't walk away a second time. I was still upset, but I'd been a damn wreck without him and knew he'd been right all along. I was his now, no matter the fight I was still willing to put up to try and resist it.

Tommy was winning with every step I made in his and Brad's direction and yet I could do nothing but go to him. He was the magnet and I was a useless clump of metal, powerless against his attractive forces pulling me in.

It'd felt like a hundred men had come onto me in that club and yet none of them had made me want them. Not even Brad, who was staring at me the same way he had just a few weeks before when he'd propositioned me for sex after filming our bathtub scene.

And then there was the guy standing next to him who looked like he wanted to swallow me whole. Darkness and light stood personified before me. Two men who were different in so many ways.

How could I want the bad man? How could I crave him when he'd hurt me and I knew he'd do it again and again if I forgave him? But I was powerless against his allure.

Weak.

His whether I admitted it or not.

"What can I get you to drink?" Brad asked me, but in all honesty, I'd already had enough.

"I'm good thanks," I replied and I came to a stop between the two of them with a coy smile. Without another word, I then raised my hands and cupped Brad's face before planting a soft kiss on his top lip. I knew he enjoyed it, but in all honesty, I was using him for appearances sake. If I'd have walked up and kissed Tommy it would've looked obvious that something was going on between us. If I kissed them both, I could argue I'd done it simply in greeting.

So, I then turned to Tommy and did the same, having to lift up onto my tiptoes to reach him. He wasn't impressed at first, I could tell, but he soon softened and by the time I pulled away, his eyes were no longer dark and scary. They were like the deepest of oceans on a hot day and I wanted to get lost in them.

I swooned and sighed. "You're here…" I whispered so Brad wouldn't hear us.

"You're mine, Piper. Where else would I be?" he answered, so matter-of-factly it made me smile.

I wanted to cry. Why couldn't he always be like this? Why did I have to endure his cruelty first before I could have his softness? Why couldn't he just love and adore me, and that be enough? Why, why, why?

Some of our friends then found us and together we all danced and drank and then danced some more. By the end of it I was smiling and laughing again. Enjoying myself and vowing to leave the past behind me.

Tommy was having fun too. I could see it in his eyes. Maybe he wanted to go back to the night beside his pool too? To start over again and not make the same mistakes.

I hoped so.

TWENTY-FOUR

Tommy

There was no going back. Not now I'd cracked it. I knew exactly how to manipulate Piper and wrap her around my little finger. It'd barely taken any effort at all really.

All I had to do was offer her the kind of love every woman craved. The doting glances and soft smiles. The promise of affection and lovemaking to come. For me to appear weakened by her was an easy role to play and she lapped it up, believing everything I was portraying.

Little did she know of the things I still had planned. No one could know the depths of my depravity. No one but her and by the time she learned the truth, it'd be too late. It already was in many respects.

It was late when we all left the club, but the party wasn't stopping so we shared a cab and headed for Brad's penthouse apartment. He'd opted for a central location rather than in Beverly Hills like Piper and me, so it made sense to take the party back to his place and I didn't mind.

Brad hadn't failed to notice I had my sights set on Piper, so luckily he'd opted to pursue her friend instead and we both ditched our buddies so we could make this a different kind of party.

We arrived and Brad delighted in showing us around his place and I had to admit, it was classier than I'd expected. Decorated with warm, neutral colors and he had nothing too showy. I liked it and could imagine myself living somewhere similar.

We grabbed some drinks from his bar and the four of us shot the shit for a while before he finally plucked up the courage to make the moves on Janie. She didn't need asking twice and practically had to drag him to his room, leaving Piper and I alone at long last.

She seemed shy with me for some strange reason, which I found amusing. Rather than put her at ease I left the awkward silence hanging in the air. Watched as she tried to come up with something to say or decide what to do. I was entranced. An overwhelming urge to punish and command her came over me. My sweet little lover and her pale blue eyes that drove me wild. Her blonde hair was begging to be pulled. Her ass spanked. Her mouth stuffed full of my cock as I gagged her on it.

I watched her as she found the perfect spot on the sofa and beckoned me over to join her, which I did. I even smiled sweetly and nestled in close.

"Do you forgive me?" I asked, turning on the charm.

"Yes," she replied with a gentle smile. "And do you forgive me for breaking your number-one rule?" As if I'd needed reminding about those goddamn tears of hers. My blood boiled at the sheer remembrance.

"Always," I lied. She wasn't forgiven. Not yet. Not until I had forced her to understand that there would always be consequences for her actions. That she wasn't free to choose, only be led.

"Maybe we can move forward and use what happened at the cabin as a lesson never to push each other so far again?" she replied hopefully. I hummed in feigned agreement, not really caring about anything other than getting what I'd come for.

"Take off your clothes," I demanded, having had enough of the talk. To my surprise, Piper did it without argument. When she was good and naked I ran my hands over her perfect breasts and supple skin. "Good, now open your legs." She complied again so I let my hand float lower down her body where I found her more than ready for me. I gave her a little strum but only for a few seconds. It wasn't time for her to receive pleasure. Not until the punishment was over and my torturous side had been locked back in his box.

I pulled my hand away and stood over her, unbuttoning my pants before releasing my dick. She stared at it longingly and I responded by slapping her directly across the face with it like I'd often seen happen in the porn I frequented. My cock was rock hard and gave the most wonderful spanking sound as it made contact, plus I was sure it had to have hurt her cheek. Piper shot up in shock and opened her mouth as if to shout at me, which was when I shoved my dick inside and thrust it to the back of her throat before she could even utter a sound. The look in her eyes told me she was raging, but I loved it. Couldn't she see that it only made me worse when she gave me the reaction I'd hoped for? Didn't she know how perfect her hatred was in these moments?

As I then started fucking her mouth, I gripped her by the hair at the back of her neck and shoved her down onto me. Piper gagged and writhed, trying to fight me, and her resistance only made me thrust harder.

When I neared my release I reduced speed and waited for the creeping sensation in my balls that told me it was time. Right before I shot my load down the back of her throat, I withdrew and replaced her mouth with my hand. It was barely two seconds before I was spurting my cum all over that pretty little face of hers. Piper was too busy gasping for breath and suppressing her gags to shield herself from me and by the time I was done, my jizz was dripping from her face and hair in clumps of glorious white goop.

"Tommy…" she breathed, but said nothing more. Piper knew not to test me.

"Don't move and don't speak to me, whore," I commanded as I stepped back, still admiring my handiwork. My art.

Another idea then sprang to mind and I reached for my cell phone to snap a photograph and capture this moment forever. The moment Piper was nothing. Used and defiled, she was just another whore. But it wasn't enough. I needed to humiliate her even more, so I looked around for inspiration, and quickly found it.

I scribbled on a notepad Brad had on the desk across the room and then handed the sheet to Piper so she could hold it up for my camera. I half expected her to object but I think she knew what would happen if she did. More punishments. More humiliation. Better to get it over with.

Click! The phone in my hand sounded and I peered down at the picture with a smile. You'd hardly be able to recognize her. Piper looked disheveled, her lips swollen and her eyes red from where she'd screwed them up so tightly as I'd pounded into her mouth. She was still dripping with my cum like some sort of bukkake situation had just taken place, and in her hands was my scrawled note. *Please forgive me, Tommy. I'll never run away again.*

I snatched the note back off her and ripped it to shreds before tossing it in the trash, and then I handed her a wet wipe and gave her the okay to get cleaned up. Piper looked so sweet and innocent as she removed all remnants of the 'whore' I'd just defiled. Her makeup came off with the rest and I felt myself calming as I watched.

Relaxing.

Forgiving.

The switch flipped itself and by the time she was done, I was on my knees before her, ready to show Piper just how much I'd missed her.

TWENTY-FIVE

Piper

"Tommy…" I whimpered but he shushed me and shuffled closer on his knees. I didn't know what to think or how to feel. I'd spent the last few days believing we were over, only to have ended up with him at that club and now this? I realized I wasn't even remotely over him. In fact, I'd let him use me in a way no man had ever done before. Part of me felt violated. As if he'd taken something I wasn't ready to give, but then the other part of me was so glad I'd been forgiven I didn't care if I had to perform the same act over and over again for him.

But surely he needed to be forgiven too? Why wasn't he saying sorry and making it up to me? And most importantly, why wasn't I demanding that he did so right away?

I knew why. Against all my instincts I was letting Tommy be in charge. He called the shots. The boss didn't concern himself with the needs of his minions, or so I thought. He'd probably never apologize and I knew I had to accept it.

"Let me take care of you now, Piper. I want to taste

you," he said, his voice pulling me from my dark reverie. He then wrenched open my legs and pulled me toward him so my hips fell from the edge of the couch, my pussy completely on show for him. I tried to scoot back, but he held me tighter, his fingers digging into the skin on my thighs while he shook his head.

"No," I groaned as he thrust two fingers inside of me, and I far from meant it. God, it felt so good to be touched. It felt like it'd been more than just a few days and I clenched around his fingers as he drove them in and out. Tommy responded by curling them forward and I cried out as his fingertips hit my g-spot. "No, stop…" I moaned again but gave so little of a fight I knew it was clear I didn't mean it. Tommy refused anyway. He latched onto my clit with his mouth and sucked hard, drawing it between his lips and then swirling around with his tongue. I bucked and arched my back, the sensation of his mouth on my core and his fingers still working their magic in that sweet spot deep within me making me crazy. He was relentless. There was no stopping or letting me go. No rest for the wicked, or so I thought. I cried out for him to stop, worried he might hurt me, but he refused me time and again, no matter when I begged. And then he fucked me like his life depended on it.

I woke up the next morning in a tangle of limbs sprawled across Brad's sofa. Tommy had me pinned to him, cradling me like his favorite stuffed animal, and the thought made me laugh. As if that man had ever had a stuffed toy in his life.

My breath against him made Tommy stir and I watched as he slowly came around as well. He looked so gentle in the morning light. Like the kindest man on earth, and while I of course knew he could be kind, he could also be so dreadfully cruel. I had to wonder if I really could love both of those sides to him. Whether I could be okay with the punishment and cruelty because I craved the love and tenderness I knew would come my way once I'd appeased his dark side. And would one side always be able to make up for the other? Maybe I'd never know.

"Stop frowning otherwise you're gonna need Botox," Tommy teased as he opened his eyes, and I immediately relaxed my face. I guessed I must've been frowning so made sure to regard my lover with nothing but the reverence he deserved. I didn't want to upset or anger him after all. The punishment from the night before had been brutal and gross, but also hot and dirty all at the same time. I didn't quite want a repeat of it just yet, but couldn't deny I hadn't hated being mouth-fucked, even if I could still feel the bruises in the back of my throat thanks to his forceful thrusts.

"Morning you two," Brad's chirpy voice plucked us from our morning-after reverie, making me jump. I grabbed the throw we'd been hiding under and wrapped it around myself in my haste to get covered up, my cheeks burning with embarrassment.

It didn't matter that Brad had seen me naked plenty of times. It wasn't appropriate now that we were no longer fucking each other. In contrast to my awkward reaction, Tommy didn't bat an eye as he stood and stretched. He was still showing his body off in all its naked glory as Janie came and joined us from the bedroom she'd shared with Bradley the night before.

"Holy crap, what a sight!" she cried, nodding approvingly rather than shy away and I had to laugh. Tommy simply offered her a wink and then grabbed his boxers and pants, which he slid on. I made a quick attempt of cleaning up the debris from our night of passion and then made a beeline for the bathroom so I could get washed up and dressed, as well as hide my shame for a few minutes before properly facing them.

When I returned, Brad had coffees on the go and Tommy was chatting away with Janie, telling her all about how he was indeed the mysterious guy who had broken my heart. I wanted to kill him. So much for us remaining a secret.

"You sure did a number on her, Tommy. What happened?" I heard Janie ask and I smiled at her. She really did have my back.

"A misunderstanding, but when I saw Piper last night I knew I had to make things up with her. It couldn't be the end," he replied, and then turned to offer me a kiss as I reached them.

"You made it up to me, hey?" I asked him in a whisper and absolutely adored the dark smile he offered me in return. We both knew exactly who had done the apologizing and it certainly wasn't him. I doubted it ever would be.

Maybe he truly was the ultimate dominant and I just hadn't realized it before? I was becoming more and more subservient to his every whim without him having to ask or demand it of me. I followed orders and took pleasure in pleasing him. I loved seeing his smile and wanted more of his affection and attention. I wanted to be a good girl and receive the rewards only he could give me. Shit, maybe I was submitting to him.

"I'm happy for you guys," Brad said as he put two coffees down in front of us and I thanked him. It was good to know there were no hard feelings. "But, I'm guessing it needs to be kept a secret until the movie promo is done, right?"

I looked to Tommy for him to answer. In all honesty, I couldn't see the harm in coming clean about our relationship, but wanted him to make the decision for the both of us. He was the star of the film and I wasn't sure what angle he'd wanted to take during the PR time in the build up to its release.

"Let's keep the news solely about the new film for now. We can come out about us when the time is right," he said and I nodded. It made sense for us to be talking about the movie and not about ourselves in the upcoming interviews. The talkshow hosts wouldn't be able to help themselves, but we weren't going to be there to discuss our private lives.

"Speaking of which," Janie interjected, "are you guys both ready?"

"Yeah, I don't have many lined up until we hit the South American schedule," Brad answered first. "I've been asked to go down the angle of adding intrigue to the plot. Reveal just a little about how intense the story is and how we tied it to the real goings on between George Ward and his many foolish minions."

I saw something flash across Tommy's face when Brad talked about George and had to wonder what it was. Perhaps anger? If so, I couldn't fathom why. He'd told me himself how George was gone. Safely tucked away just like the other characters he had played over the years, so wasn't sure why Tommy would be angered by Brad talking about him with a hint of distaste in this tone. They weren't really the mobster and his henchman. The pair of them were simply two actors who I had assumed to be friends, but perhaps I was wrong?

Thankfully Janie and Brad had been chatting amongst themselves about what she'd been informed the producers wanted from me during the interviews. They were engrossed in their conversation, while I watched as a shudder swept over Tommy. And then, quick as a flash, he was back to his usual self again. Well, the persona he adopted for everyone except me, or so it seemed. His happy go lucky way and cocky grin were back, but when he turned to me, I saw the iciness in his stare. The sheer and total detachment.

"I have to go," he said. "I'll call you."

"Okay," I replied, offering him a smile I knew didn't reach my eyes. I couldn't tell what was going on with him, but I knew something was up. I just had to hope he might one day open up to me and reveal all. Even if it meant opening up that Pandora's box inside of him that kept his demons at bay.

He left and I sat watching Bradley and Janie talk for a while, offering a bit to the conversation here and there but I was lost in my own thoughts again. Worrying about whether Tommy was okay and whether or not I should go and see him.

"I think it's time we went home too," Janie eventually told Brad, and while I was glad, I could tell he was a little disappointed to be saying goodbye. Maybe they'd had more fun together than I'd realized? Maybe even more than just a one-night stand? I knew Janie would tell me all about it when we got out of there so I gathered up my things, checked I looked presentable enough, and then went out in the hall to call a town car, having chosen one I'd used numerous times before and trusted not to tip off the paparazzi.

When we got back to my place I was barely in the door before Janie began spilling the beans. "Listen, I know you two used to hook up and of course that's fine by me but I need to know something. You're okay with me sleeping with him aren't you?"

"Of course!" I cried. I hadn't cared at all, if I was honest. If anything, it was nice to see how neither she nor Brad had been surprised by me and Tommy hooking up. It made me hope for the same reaction from the masses if and when we decided to go public with our relationship. "Tommy and I are really becoming something so the stuff with Brad is ancient history. God, I remember thinking it was just gonna be a bit of fun between me and him. It scares me but at the same time I can't get enough."

"Yeah. I was going to ask you about him," she replied, her face turning serious. "I heard you two last night. Some of the things you were saying to each other had me a little concerned…"

I felt a wave of dread wash over me. What had we been saying? Nothing I could remember that would be too incriminating, surely?

"Like what?" I croaked.

"You were telling him no but he didn't stop…"

Relief flooded my system. I let out a soft sigh and leaned closer to her, wanting Janie to understand and believe me when I told her my reply.

"It's just one of those things I like to do, you know, when in the throes of passion? He knows I don't mean it so keeps going." I had to admit, she did look relieved and I was glad. The last thing I needed was for my closest friend to think I was getting into something dangerous or was out of my depth with Tommy. Well, maybe I was, but she didn't need to know that.

"Brad said the same when I asked him if I should come out and check on you. He said you used to do it with him too—"

"The less said about that, the better I think," I interjected and Janie laughed.

"Yeah," she agreed, "but just as long as you're okay now and aren't in any trouble?"

"I'm great and couldn't be further from trouble, trust me." I wasn't sure Janie believed me, but then again I couldn't be all that sure I believed myself.

TWENTY-SIX

Tommy

I slept for a while when I got home and my dreams were full of her. They were dark dreams. Full of lustful drives and me succumbing to the violent urges I fought every day in my waking moments. I eventually woke with a raging hard-on that was clearly going nowhere so I turned to my new favorite website. After logging into the members' only area I sifted through the new recordings and found the perfect accompaniment to my afternoon jerk-off session.

My laptop screen went dark for a second before the file opened with the image of a young woman being tied to a bed by her ankles and wrists. She was crying real tears. No one could fake those, so I turned my face away and waited until her captor covered her eyes with a black mask. Perfect.

"Perfect," he said, mirroring my thoughts and I smiled. I knew exactly what I was going to invest in next. Behind a mask Piper could cry all she wanted and I'd could ignore her. I'd be able to take things further than before and my one debilitating issue wouldn't necessarily be so much of a problem thanks to a mask that could hide it all away.

The punisher on the screen then whipped and beat the girl before my eyes. She wasn't one of those masochists who took pleasure in the pain, but evidently a real and everyday person who cried and pleaded for it to stop. But it didn't matter. He wouldn't stop no matter what she did, and I loved it. I caressed my cock in one hand and began stroking up and down, tightening my grip every time she screamed. It was heaven.

When the man on the screen parted her thighs and stroked the woman's pussy, she tried to fight him off but it was no use. He was inside of her a second later, pummeling hard. When he was done, he withdrew and came all over her stomach and then was right back inside of her, ready for more. After he'd come a second time, he then started beating her again and I lost my damn mind watching her flinch and hearing cry out.

Pleasure and torture were working side-by-side rather than exclusive to one another. The concept of not just doing it once but over and over again in one sitting sent me over the edge. My eyes were closed and I could envision Piper at my mercy. The cries I could hear on screen were hers. The loud grunts of her tormentor mine. My hand was pumping hard on my cock and with a loud cry I then came into the tissue I'd had at the ready.

I knew what I had to do. But not yet. Piper was still getting over what I'd done at the cabin so I decided I had to tread carefully. Bide my time.

I shut off the video and logged out of the website, and deleted my browsing history for good measure before shutting down. As I lay back on my bed and stared up at the ceiling, all I could picture was Piper tied to that bed and me over her, punishment fucking to the sound of her screams.

I needed to get away from that fantasy rather than indulge it, I knew. Instead of jerking off again I decided to go for a run. I went on my usual route and then doubled back on myself, detouring through Piper's neighborhood because I simply couldn't resist taking a peek at my darling girl. Perhaps I would find her in a compromising position worthy of severe punishment… A guy could dream, hey?

She was in her living room by the window doing her yoga routine in nothing but her underwear. Her body was curling and stretching in a stunning and obviously well practiced set of moves and I watched for a few glorious minutes. I couldn't go inside and take her, not in the mood I was in, so instead I crept away and hightailed it for home.

There, I found the front door ajar. I was sure I'd locked it when I'd left, but still went straight in. I wasn't afraid to confront an intruder and went inside to rather than head for the phone to call the security guards that myself and the other homeowners in our cul-de-sac paid handsomely to stop this very thing from happening.

I took a look around the ground floor. Nothing looked out of place and there wasn't anything missing so I went room to room in search of a clue as to who might've snuck into my home. As I rounded the top of the stairs to the first floor, I found my answer.

Soft humming was coming from the master bathroom. I could hear a bath running inside and saw steam slowly escaping from beneath the closed door. My intruder was taking a bath. How delightful.

With a wolfish grin I crept closer, and knew who it was before I'd even laid eyes on her.

Regardless of the restraining order against her and the numerous times I had told her to leave me alone, my stalker had returned to me. Marina Del Rey had been obsessed with me for years and had become a joke to my friends and me. Someone I despised for being so weak and vulnerable when it came to her girlish whimsy. She was so desperate to please me and have me love her that she'd resorted to overly exaggerated declarations of love and adoration over the years.

I'd enjoyed the attention at first. Even the late night

messages on my cell when she'd begged one of the crewmembers on set for my number. Then there were her numerous gifts and of course her being frontline in the crowd at all of my red-carpet appearances. I'd thought she was harmless, but not when her adoration had turned to bothersome obsession.

The last time I saw Marina was when she'd broken into my home and tried to seduce me. I might've been desperate enough to fuck her, if only she hadn't crept into my bedroom in the dead of night and basically tried to rape me. After that, Marina was no longer considered just a harmless fanatic. She'd had to be stopped and my efforts to remove her from my life had seemed to work. Until now.

I knew it couldn't be Piper in there either. I was the one who stalked her and had crept into her home unannounced, not the other way around. Plus, I'd just been watching her so knew she was home working out and not in my bathroom getting ready to take a dip in my tub.

I turned the handle and stalked inside. Marina jumped right out of her skin and leapt to her feet. Her face was sour, as if she'd been expecting a fight, but as soon as she saw me smiling she softened and beamed at me. I eyed her up and down. Marina was stark naked and she liked having my eyes on her, I could tell. If only she knew how I detested the sight before me. Her tiny little tits were doing nothing to entice my flaccid cock, and neither was her scrawny waist and bare cunt. I was about to tell her to get the hell out of my house, when she broke the silence.

"I couldn't stay away any longer, Tommy," she drawled. "The doctors tried to break me with their words and meds but I couldn't listen or take them any longer. Not when I knew they were mistaken. My love for you isn't wrong, it's just different. Let me show you how much I love you. I'll do anything you want. Be whatever you need," Marina added.

She then fell to her knees before me, staring up into my

eyes like a loyal, dutiful servant ready to do whatever her master commanded.

"Anything?" I enquired, my smile turning salacious.

"Anything…" she drawled, clearly aiming for seductive when in fact the sound had the opposite effect on me. However, there were some things she could assist me with.

A dozen ideas went through my mind. Perhaps I could tie her up and beat her? Re-enact any of the numerous violent porn movies I'd been watching of late? Piper would never have to know and Marina could help me curb those desires welling within me that I didn't dare let loose on my main girl. I opened my mouth to speak and was about to command that she go to my bedroom and wait for me, but right at the last second I changed my mind. If I fucked Marina I knew I couldn't live with knowing I'd betrayed Piper. If I beat her and left her unsatisfied in the aftermath Marina might go running to the gossip columns to sell her story and ruin me. My only option was to do as I had always done and send her away.

"Then leave and don't come back. If I find you in my house again you won't like how I react." I stepped back and went to turn away, which was when I saw the flash of metal in the light and whipped back to face her. I'd expected a knife or something, but all she had in her grasp was a small shard of metal that looked like a piece from one of those crafting knives they used on set when creating elaborate effects in makeup.

"Please," Marina begged, holding the blade in the center of her wrist as though she might be about to slit it. "I need you, Tommy. If I can't have you then I might as well be dead." Her hand hovered over the veins there, poised as though she might actually do it, and as I stood watching in shock, something inside of me exploded in intrigue.

I wanted her to do it. I wanted to watch. For the first time in all the years I'd known Marina, I felt desirous of her. Not of her body in a carnal way like with Piper, but something else. Something entirely darker.

I reached out and put one hand under her wrist to hold the exposed arm steady, and the other on the trembling hand with the blade in it. Marina sighed in relief, like she thought I was going to take the blade away and change my mind about making her leave. Her foolish trust in me only made my dark heart beat faster.

Do it, a voice in my head demanded. *It'll look like a suicide.*

And so, I pushed the two together: the blade and her delicate forearm. She let out a cry as the metal pierced her skin and I felt her try to pull out of my grasp as if she was suddenly rethinking her promise to do anything I demanded, but it was no use. Her tiny body was nothing in comparison to mine and with no effort on my part at all I yanked the blade up her inner forearm in one delectable and incredibly deep slice.

I then let go and with a shriek Marina threw the blade to the ground. We both stared at the cut for a second as her blood rose up into the groove and then began to pour out onto the floor. I watched in fascination as she processed what was happening and then cringed as she began to sob.

"If you can't have me then you'd rather be dead, huh?" I reminded her, stepping away as she fell to her knees, looking paler by the second. "Then die," I whispered, watching her as my dark smile returned. "Die for me, Marina."

I thought she might try to save herself or run, but she didn't. Marina really was broken. Too broken to fight for her life any longer. She just stayed there on the ground, bleeding out, and breathed a deep sigh.

"Tell me you love me, Tommy. Tell me I'm beautiful," she whimpered, watching me through eyes that were growing steadily glassier.

"You're beautiful, Marina. Look at you," she followed my gaze down to the crimson pool forming around her and let out a dry laugh. "Thank you for giving me your life. I love you," I then said, and she smiled to herself.

Marina was still smiling when she slumped against the side of the bath and stopped breathing. I didn't need to check her pulse to know she'd gone. She was pale and floppy, unmoving, and all I wanted to do was watch her lifeless body sit there by my tub. I was in awe. Mesmerized by what'd just happened. Turned on by it.

I replayed the final moments of Marina's life in my mind. I'd done it. I'd made the cut that'd killed her, willing or not. I was a murderer.

And then it suddenly hit me. I was a murderer!

I ran to the toilet and threw up into it. What had I done? How could I have gone through with such a heinous act? I deserved to go to jail for what I'd made her do and knew I owed it to Marina to call the cops and admit to what I'd done.

But then again, maybe not. I wasn't that righteous. She'd wanted this after all. I hadn't taken the life of an innocent. Why should I pay for what she herself had done?

After I'd finished puking my guts up I cleaned my face and went out into the hall where I stood and stared out the window at the top of the stairs. It was dark out and I could see my reflection in it. I looked a wreck.

This is good, I thought. *Use it…*

I grabbed my cell from the bedroom and dialed up Miles. He answered after the first ring.

"Hey," he said.

"Hey, man. I need your help. Something's happened," I replied before I then proceeded to tell Miles how I'd come home from my run and found Marina dead in my bathroom. Yes, I was a murderer, but I certainly wasn't going to come clean. If there was a high road, I certainly didn't intend on taking it.

The cops arrived after Miles had come to inspect the scene for himself. He seemed convinced I was telling the truth and so had called the police as well as my lawyer, just in case.

The first responders also came along but there was nothing any of them could do other than wait for the coroner to arrive and do their thing. I gave my statement and acted shocked and horrified by what had happened, which was further proven when the forensics team found my vomit in the toilet.

"I couldn't believe what I was seeing at first, but when it finally sunk in, I was sick to my stomach. I'm sorry," I told the deputy taking down my story, but he waved me away.

"It's okay, a lot of people react the same way to finding a dead body. It's nothing you ever get used to," he said and I nodded.

The police stayed for hours and by the time they left I was exhausted. I showered in my en-suite and climbed into bed, but couldn't sleep. Marina's death kept replaying in my head but that wasn't what was keeping me awake. It was the questions. What if I'd missed something? What if they didn't believe my story and looked into the case a little deeper? Would they figure me out? Would I cave and tell them the truth? Would I end up spending my life in prison or eventually find myself on death row?

With a curse I turned onto my side and grabbed my cell. There were a barrage of messages on there thanks to the police presence having tipped off the press so I'd put it on silent hours previously, but the most recent text was from the one person I knew could calm me and I was glad to hear from her.

Piper:
I can't stop thinking of you. Are you okay?

I hit the call button and put it to my ear, rather than text her back.

"Hey," her voice came through the speaker and she

sounded husky, like she'd been asleep.

"Where are you?" I asked, turning onto my back and staring at the ceiling.

"In bed but I haven't been able to sleep. I keep thinking about what happened and whether you're okay."

"I'm fine," I lied. "She was someone who was unhinged and had broken into my home. I don't know why she did what she did, but I just hope everything's cleared up soon."

"Me too. When will I get to see you again?" she asked, and I heard her voice falter. Was she worried? Did she miss me? God, I hoped so. In fact, I damn right expected her to.

"Close your eyes and touch yourself, beautiful girl. I'm there with you. Can you feel me?"

I heard Piper let out a soft moan and knew she was doing exactly as I'd asked when she started panting and groaning. "Yes, that's it." I grabbed my cock and started to move with her. In my mind's eye I could envision Piper lying strewn over her bed, rubbing her delicious cunt. I imagined myself standing over her to watch as she strummed on her clit and when she began crying out in orgasm, I released as well.

"Tommy," she then whimpered, still panting. "Are you still there?"

"Yeah, I'm here," I replied as I cleaned myself up. I was about to tell her goodnight, but instead a moment of need washed over me and I asked her for something I hadn't needed or asked anyone for in a long time. I asked her to tell me it was all going to be okay.

"You're going to be fine, Tommy," she said. "That poor girl wasn't right in the head and she did something foolish because of it. You're not to blame."

If only she knew the truth. I was to blame. I had murdered Marina and while I strangely felt no remorse any more, I was still terrified I might get caught. No part of me was ready for prison or to lose the life I had made for myself.

"You're right," I eventually whispered back. "Thank you." I then said goodnight and ended the call before tossing my cell onto the bedside table. *So, Marina*, I thought. *We're going to keep this our little secret.*

I fell asleep quickly after that, my resolve to focus on self-preservation above all things helping to stop the voices screaming in my head.

TWENTY-SEVEN

Piper

Tommy ended up pretty much unreachable for days following Marina's suicide and I hated that I couldn't be with him. We talked on the phone plenty, but I could never quite figure out whether I thought he was actually okay or if he was just saying so. He seemed to not really care all that much about what Marina had done and I couldn't understand why. I knew he wasn't heartless and yet every time I asked how he was dealing with things he just batted my concern away like he truly didn't care enough to want to talk about what'd happened. I eventually figured it was all part of his coping mechanism and decided to stop asking altogether.

I spent the time reading through the script for the new movie I'd decided to audition for and used the alone time to practice my lines. Our promo dates were also rapidly approaching and while things had been re-jigged a little to accommodate Tommy's crazy schedule, I was more than ready to get going with promoting *Wayward.* I was excited to see the end product too and when I got the call from Janie to say the screener had arrived, I asked her to bring it right over. She was at my house less than thirty minutes later and we immediately sat down to watch the DVD she'd had delivered by courier just an hour or so before.

The movie began and I watched as 'George' dominated the scenes with his intimidating way. That truly wasn't Tommy and I understood at last just how different he became when playing his roles. There were snippets of the real him here and there, though. Looks and mannerisms that I'd come to know and love in him, but mostly he had been transformed. George Ward through and through. I watched in intrigue as my own scenes with Brad then came on screen and couldn't say I hated any of them. The bath scene had been shot well and I didn't feel I was too exposed or the scene itself indecent. In fact, it was pretty damn hot and I felt like it accurately portrayed the love Brad and I had tried to demonstrate effectively between the two characters.

And then came my sex scene with George. I had a feeling viewers were either going to love it or hate it based on their stances on infidelity and such, but overall I felt like it was probably the hottest thing I had ever seen. By the end of it I was blushing and I turned to find Janie looking a little flush herself. In all honesty, Tommy had some sex scenes with Scarlet that were way hotter than ours in a visual perspective, but something about what we'd managed to portray on the screen seemed more intense to me. Like it had truly been a wondrous and intimate moment between two people rather than something scripted or planned. I loved it, but was also worried it might be too strong. That it could end up denting my reputation rather than improve it.

I waited until the whole movie was over before looking to Janie for her reaction, but I couldn't deny I was desperately anxious to find out what she'd thought about it. I myself was pleased. *Wayward* was far grittier than anything I'd worked on before and the intense scenes were explosive and exciting, while the romantic elements had ranged from sexy and smooth to hot and dark.

"So… what do you think?" I eventually asked when I could bite my tongue no longer.

"What do I think?" Janie replied, her mouth hanging open in shock. "I think this is the movie that's gonna make you, Piper. This is an incredible take on an age-old story of the gangster and the girl that's been done time and again, but you guys made it into something truly incredible. I felt like I was a fly on the wall watching real life rather than a storyline based loosely on facts someone sat and wrote at a computer one day."

I breathed a huge sigh of relief and wrung my hands. God, I hoped she was right. I felt really good in spite of my fear of ruining my image, but Janie was right. The movie was great. I'd taken a risk and a calculated one too, but I had to believe it was going to pay off. That it'd be worth it.

"I'm shaking," I told her and she put an arm around me.

"That's because you want this, Piper. You deserve it and I can't wait to see what everyone else's reaction is of this amazing movie."

I couldn't speak. I didn't dare to hope that this film coming out might just be the pivotal moment in my career, but couldn't help it. There were so many things I wanted for myself and in life in general, but I felt like maybe, just maybe, I was finally on the road to getting all of those things.

TWENTY-EIGHT

Tommy

I tried not to watch it. Like with all my work, I didn't like to see myself on screen, but this time was different. I was getting to watch *her*. To see us in our perfect scene atop that kitchen counter and I found myself enjoying all the parts Piper was in no matter of how obvious it was that she was still nothing more than one of the supporting cast members. Don't get me wrong, I thought of her far differently after our time together to when I'd turned up on set that first day, and I was sure the viewing public were going to think of her differently after seeing this movie too.

But then, something snapped inside of me as I watched her fuck Brad in that bathtub. I know she said nothing happened for real, but could I ever really be sure? It looked real enough and I'd heard the chatter on set about how they'd discarded their modesty covers and been bumping uglies all day long. I knew how easy it would've been for him to slip inside and for Piper to take a real ride. It wasn't uncommon at all and I knew plenty of actors who got off on knowing they'd done it for real in front of not only the crew and other cast members on filming day, but then again to countless viewers who would watch the movie later on.

Was Brad one of those people? Had he bragged to others about how he'd fucked Piper on camera and elicited an apparent climax while I had only rubbed her to orgasm during our own?

I had to know, but also to let him know he couldn't get away with taking what was mine. She had already belonged to me when they'd shot that scene and violent rage simmered within me for long after their scene had finished.

I watched the movie till the end but my mind was elsewhere. I was thinking of Piper fondly, but also remembering Marina's death with disgust. And then another thought kept creeping in around the edges of that distaste. What would I do differently if I had the chance? Would I make her death quicker or slower? More or less gory and gruesome? At first I wasn't sure, but then I started to imagine not just slashing her one wrist, but the other too. Maybe I'd wait and watch the blood some more. I closed my eyes and imagined myself holding her arms high so the blood streamed down her arms and body, coating her in a sort of dark and vivid ink while the rest of the color faded from her skin. I thought about that over and over, never caring for the life lost but of how she would've looked if I'd only stopped and properly taken it in. If I'd thought to savor the moment she had given me.

That was when it struck me.

I could just try again.

Do it a second time and use the lessons I'd learned from Marina's death to perfect the second. But who would I choose as my next nominee? Not a Marina lookalike. She didn't turn me on in the slightest, but maybe a small, blonde beauty with a face naturally innocent and wide blue eyes…

She'd do nicely.

Just like my Piper, I would take her in my arms and kiss her, but unlike with my girl, I wouldn't fuck this one. I would kill her. And when it was all over, I would let myself into Piper's home and fuck her instead, whether she wanted me to or not because, even though she wouldn't know it, I would've just killed for her.

I fell asleep after a night spent all up in my head. Between my dreams of deviant murder and watching snuff films on my new favorite website I had to have jerked off twenty times, but I didn't regret a thing or feel ashamed of a single moment of it. In fact, part of me wanted to share the euphoria I was filled with.

I considered going to see Piper and telling her all about what I'd done and still wanted to do. How I wanted to kill in her name. In my fantasy, she would smile and tell me yes—do it. The only thing stopping me was that I didn't really know if she would understand. I couldn't know for sure and decided that instead of turning my hand to murder, I'd focus instead on punishing her for not only what I'd had to watch on that screen between her and Brad, but also for her not being ready to hear my innermost desires. She owed it to me to be ready and yet there she still was, thinking I even gave a flying fuck about that scrawny bitch whose blood would always leave its mark on my home.

I rolled out of bed and into the shower. It was time for me to finally leave the house and face the cameras for the first time since Marina had died in my tub. The police had already been by to tell me the case was closed so I knew there wouldn't—or shouldn't—be any suspicion of me, but I still knew the questions would come. Everyone would want to know the story so when I was dressed and ready, I took a moment to call upon a voice from somewhere deep within me. One I had locked away with all the others, but who was being unleashed for the time being to help me remain convincing in my lies. I stood in front of the mirror and softened my stare while I let my brows relax. I then took a few deep breaths and then cleared my throat.

"Mental health is something we should all talk about," I said over and over again, trying out different sounds until I found a tone of voice I was sure would sound sincere. "Suicide affects everyone close to the victim and I can't deny, it hasn't been easy saying goodbye to Marina. I only wish she'd let me help her."

When my lines were rehearsed to perfection, I offered my reflection a wicked grin and then sauntered away. I knew I had it figured out. In the fucking bag.

***

The three days that followed were nothing more than a constant stream of interviews with people from magazines and radio shows or small-time TV stations. I said the same lines over and over. Answered the same questions over and over. The only thing that kept me sane was knowing that Piper was close by. Sometimes she was in the same room as me for joint interviews between us two and Scarlet and we'd all banter and chat away about *Wayward* like old pals. Other times, she'd be in another room giving private interviews and I could hear her laughing or shrieking in delight at whatever weird and wonderful things those interviewing her could come up with.

I was asked relentlessly about Marina but did the same thing each time—delivered my practiced lines and used that soft and gentle tone of voice I was beginning to hate. The interviewers lapped it up every damn time. Fuckwits.

After the main elements of smaller PR were done, it was time for the big ones. The chat shows with billions of viewers or the comedy shows where myself and Scarlet parodied the movie via skits and piss-takes. Piper didn't attend those. The producers had specifically asked for the two leading actors and no one else and I hated that she wasn't with me as I travelled from studio to studio, and even across the country for appearances in the cities of New York, Philadelphia and Boston.

Piper was there when it mattered though. Scarlet had just had surgery for some made-up disease she apparently had and was hit and miss as to whether she was well enough to do the appearances. I couldn't give any less of a shit about Scarlet and made that clear to the only person I knew wouldn't care—Miles. I often wondered if he was like me. He certainly had that same edge to his humor I did and when we were alone our jokes often became so depraved in nature that I was sure I could see a glimpse of his darkness. But more to the point, he could also see mine. And yet, neither of us pulled away from our friendship, which was all the confirmation either of us needed.

I immediately informed Piper of Scarlet's lack of commitment and she had the forethought to be the first to offer to tag along with us under the pretense of being there solely for the benefit of the movie's PR should Scarlet be too poorly to feature on whatever show we were lined up to do. It worked and before I knew it, she was travelling right along with us. Deep down, she was just as devious as me and I loved her all the more for it.

It was manic, though. Every night we were both too exhausted to play any of our usual games but we always shared either her bed or mine in whatever hotel we'd been put up in. It was the first time I'd ever truly made love to a woman, and for twelve nights straight we did the same routine over and over again. I didn't feel the need to punish her any more, only to give and take as much pleasure as I was able, and I could tell she liked having things back to some semblance of simplicity between us. I couldn't get enough and would've been inside her for hours every night if I could. I tried, but Piper wasn't as strong as I was. There were times when she couldn't keep up with me. When she told me no and I knew she meant it, but I still didn't stop. She would whimper as I pressed against her opening and I knew it was on the tip of her tongue to tell me not to go any further, but each and every time I dived right on in. Within seconds she was always wet for me and on board, and the darkness deep down inside of me loved forcing her to obey my desires.

I got her drunk again the first night of our European PR dates. We had the following morning off to allow for jetlag and she was struggling to adjust to the time change so I suggested a few drinks to help take the edge off. That way she could try and get some sleep regardless of what her body was telling her. Piper fell right into my trap. The concierge brought us up a bottle of champagne in an ice bucket and this time, I joined her for a few before saying I was switching to the whiskey from the small chiller our rooms all came with. I poured myself miniscule shots over water and ice while Piper was giggling and falling about drunk before she'd even finished the first bottle. I knew it was time to do as I'd done the last night like this. I had to force myself into her mind. Make her think solely of me and be willing to do whatever it took to protect what we had.

"You'll stand by me through anything, won't you?" I asked as I pulled her into my arms and began undressing her. "Be my rock. Have my back…"

"What do you mean, baby?" she replied with a frown.

"Like, if I did a bad thing. Would you join the others in persecuting me, or would you stand by me?"

"I don't know!" she cried and I let her go, watching as she refilled her glass and took a swig. "What would you do that was so bad?"

"Nothing," my voice was low and hoarse. I stepped closer to her, capturing Piper in my grasp and in my stare. "And that's precisely my point. I could never do anything wrong or bad. That's what I mean, Piper. I need you to always believe it. To be ready to tell others the same."

"You're not the bad guy anyway," she said, swaying on her feet.

My whole body went tense and I felt a wave of ice cold shudders trickle up and down my spine. She wasn't understanding what I was getting at and it irked me to no end. I charged toward her and saw Piper flinch. Damn that made me hard.

"I thought you said I wasn't the bad guy?" I croaked as I plucked the champagne flute from her hand and placed it down.

"You're not," Piper implored me, but I was having none of it. It was time she learned to stop thinking for herself and think the way I did. The way I let her think.

She then let out a gasp as I tore the rest of her clothes away and lifted her up into my arms, linking her ankles around my back. I shoved Piper against the wall and covered her mouth with mine.

"No, I'm not the bad guy," I then groaned against her lips. "You need to remember that always. Never forget it or deny the facts, because I love you and never want to leave you. No matter what… But right now, you're being a bad girl and bad girls need to be punished."

Piper flinched again and this time, I saw real fear in her eyes. She was finally learning about my punishments and how I meant business when it came to administering them. But I wanted more. I needed for her to forget everything other than me. For her to think the same thoughts as I did. Have the same opinions as me and never deviate from whatever plan I dictated.

"What are you going to do?" she whimpered.

"I'm going to humiliate you somehow," I replied after thinking on it for a second or two. I wasn't sure how or when, but I was going to make sure she understood just what it meant to follow not only my rules, but my unwritten and sometimes unspoken law to do as I said and please me without fail. Was this love? I couldn't know, but I did know I had to control her and exert that control over her any time I feasibly could.

"Why?" she replied timidly and I shook my head.

"You know why." She peered up at me with doe eyes through her long blonde lashes and shook her head. Perhaps she wasn't quite there yet after all, which only made me surer that she needed her punishment. "Because you made me love you, dammit. You made me care and that makes me weak. And I cannot be weak." I fixed Piper with a dark stare and shoved myself harder against her, taking her breath away—literally.

I kissed and stroked at her naked body for a while but could wait no longer and simply had to have her. Piper let me take her anyway I wanted. I threw her around that hotel room like a ragdoll and she loved every minute of it. My girl might've been a little unsure of whether she could handle my darkness, but she was certainly starting to embrace her own and I loved her even more for it.

TWENTY-NINE

Piper

We woke late after our first night in London but I felt reasonably rested in spite of the muscles in my legs and arms screaming as I stretched them. Tommy and I had been working out so hard between the sheets lately that I'd neglected my usual yoga routine and in spite of the slight hangover churning my stomach, I decided to get up and do my sun salutation.

In nothing but my underwear, I climbed out of bed and began moving through the sequence I'd done hundreds of times since finding my favorite method of working out. It felt good, even when the top of my thighs smarted a little thanks to being sore.

I did the routine over and over and got steadily quicker, and by the time I was done, a light sheen of sweat covered me from head to toe. That was when I turned and found Tommy watching me from the bed. A memory of the night before snapped into the forefront of my mind and part of me wanted to ask him about what he had in store for my punishment, but I also didn't dare. Knowing Tommy, he would make it ten times worse if I pushed him on the subject. I wasn't even all that sure why I was due a punishment, but I didn't ask him about that either. Instead I simply smiled at him.

"How long have you been watching me?" I asked.

"I'm always watching, Piper. You know I like to watch. In fact, I believe you caught me once or twice," he replied, licking his lips as he eyed me up and down.

"Well, if I wasn't completely sure you made a habit of lurking in my bushes then I am now," I teased before checking my watch. "It's almost time to go."

"Ah yes, the joys of daytime television followed by some kind of comedy show," he said, following me into the bathroom. I laughed and turned to him.

"You've never seen it?" I asked and he shook his head. "Well, I don't always get the British humor but I have to admit, it's a damn funny show. They're gonna give you one hell of a time, baby."

Tommy didn't seem impressed with my offhand comment.

"What do you mean by that?" he demanded, but rather than cower timidly, something inside of me resisted the urge to let him dominate me. I knew I'd been letting him take charge more and more, but hadn't realized we'd gotten to the point where he really was becoming more than just overbearing. He was trying to intimidate me to where I felt I was no longer myself.

That wouldn't do, so I stood taller and met his hard stare.

"You heard me," I said. "They'll ask you the usual questions but be prepared to go off the scripted answers. They'll want to hear something funny or intriguing while trying to get you to slip up on something random for the fun of it."

Tommy shrugged and then backed off, much to my surprise. I then saw his cheeky grin return and I was reminded of the first afternoon we'd spent together in his hot tub. I missed the banter we'd thrown one another's way that day. Before I'd seen that darkness flash behind his eyes and for some reason welcomed it with open arms. Part of me wondered if I'd live to regret that moment. If I'd come to see that his demons were better to be locked away rather than coaxed to the surface.

I found myself constantly teetering back and forth on that thought. Sometimes I liked it and had forgiven Tommy for all the bad things he'd done, and then other times I felt rage boil beneath my skin towards him. I'd have walked away ten times already if I'd let myself, but there was always something that dragged me back. A force within him that I was drawn to like a magnet.

He barely spoke for the rest of the afternoon and seemed thoughtful. Distant. I accompanied him during the interview on some kind of daytime show I can't say was a chore. The British hosts were lovely and had us both laughing as we chatted about the movie in a far less formal interview to the type I was used to.

That evening was the comedy show. I hadn't been invited to talk on that one so I waited backstage, watching via a stream being fed directly into the greenroom as Tommy ran through his rehearsed lines and then played along when the host began to improvise.

"Come on, there had to have been one funny story from on set of any of your movies? An embarrassing anecdote you can exclusively reveal?" he asked and Tommy positively beamed. My blood ran cold. I saw it coming before Tommy had even opened his mouth and reached for my cell, ready to call Janie and get myself booked onto the next flight out of London she could find.

Tommy was laughing, acting all coy as he squirmed under the host's scrutiny. He opened his mouth as though to answer but then closed it again and shook his head.

"No, I can't," he replied, his face turning red. I'd think he was cute if I weren't already furious. Was this going to be my punishment he'd promised was coming my way for a crime I wasn't sure I'd even committed? It sure seemed like it. Even though he was playing it cool, Tommy was about to say something to incriminate me somehow. I just knew it. He was about to humiliate me like he'd promised.

"Ooh this must be good! Look at you, you're practically bouncing in your seat!" the host teased again, playing with Tommy. But I knew how it was the opposite. Tommy was in control. It was my bad, bad man who had the upper hand. He knew exactly what he was doing and something told me he'd probably planned it all along.

"Okay, but you're all gonna look at a certain someone a little differently afterwards…"

"Don't keep us in suspense," the man pleaded. I watched with bated breath as Tommy shuffled a little closer and lowered his voice, which didn't matter because he was mic'd up, but he knew that. It was all for effect.

"Well, I've done a few steamy scenes in my time and being a red-blooded man I can honestly say they got my blood pumping—if you know what I mean?" Tommy was met with a look of shock before the host then burst out laughing.

"So you… you know, were happy to see whichever female actress it was?" he asked, offering a wink to the audience.

"Oh yes!" Tommy joked. I let out a sigh, hoping that was going to be the end of it. I should've known better. "Put it this way, there was a bit of cleaning up to do after the director shouted cut."

"Oh my goodness, so what did you do?" the man then asked incredulously.

"Asked her to give me minute to calm down and then I got one of the crew to pass me a tissue." He cringed and made a wiping motion with his hand, looking embarrassed. I didn't buy it for a minute. Tommy wasn't even the slightest bit uncomfortable. He loved the attention and wouldn't have surprised me if he'd added more to the story for the fun of it.

Laughter broke out from both the audience and the

other talk show guests. They'd clearly loved his story and I just had to pray that was going to be the end of it.

"So, just which leading lady might it be who got you so hot under the collar, Mr. Darke?" he was asked, and thankfully Tommy shook his head and refused to say. Yes, he'd revealed more than he should but as it stood he wasn't in any dangerous territory. Anything more and he was liable to tarnish both our careers.

"All I can say is that she handled it with gentleness and a sense of grace that warmed me."

Wow, he was pushing his luck. He'd actually just given away who it was by outright saying my surname, and yet none of them seemed to have noticed.

Regardless of him having just paid me a compliment whilst still humiliating me, I was ready to throttle him. I had to hide all of this of course, because the damn greenroom was full of other people either watching the show or waiting for it to be over so they could get out of there. I was beginning to feel that way too.

I figured I didn't need to stay, though. My contractual obligation was to step in if Scarlet couldn't make it and there she was, sitting next to Tommy all perfect and smiling sweetly while letting him do all of the talking. She was probably only doing it because she couldn't understand the host's British accent. Yes, I was being decidedly petty and I didn't care one little bit.

I stood and headed for the door, making some blasé comment about going for some air. One of the team escorted me outside and he hovered beside me, watching me like he thought I was about to light up or something.

"What?" I demanded, making him jump. "I just wanted some air, okay."

"Of course, Miss Grace," he replied, looking sheepish.

"Unless, do you have a cigarette?" I hadn't smoked in years, but the urge to take a drag was suddenly good and strong. The young guy nodded and plucked a pack from his pocket, offering me one. I shook my head. "I just want a little bit. You have one and I'll steal a few drags."

"Sure," he said, seeming calmer around me in an instant. I eyed him up and down. He was kinda cute in an awkward, reserved way. His dark blond hair was swept to one side and brushed up into a quaff and I could tell he'd taken the time in getting himself ready for the day's work. He didn't seem the type of guy to lie in until late and then throw on the first outfit he found while rushing out the door.

"What's your name?"

"Dylan."

"And what's your job here, Dylan?"

"I'm one of Mr. Washington's assistants. We're tasked with a bit of all sorts."

"Like accompanying strays?" I teased, earning myself a small laugh. He nodded, offering me the smoke. I took it and had a small puff. It hit my throat and I inhaled, feeling the instant gratification as the euphoria hit. I had another drag before handing it back to him. "So what's really good to do around here, Dylan? Something I won't get noticed doing."

He hesitated, weighing my strange request up. Had I just asked for drugs? A place to get my rocks off? Dylan was clearly trying to figure out what, so I gave him a hint. "I like to party, Dylan. But I like it even more when people are naked. Is there anything like that in this city?" I don't know what came over me asking such a thing, maybe it was the thrill of almost getting revealed as Tommy's on-screen paramour, but I wanted something else to give me a high. Something Tommy wasn't going to be in control of.

"There are a few places, yeah," Dylan said. He offered me the cigarette again but I declined and he took the last few drags before stubbing it out and then tossing it into a nearby pail already half-full of butts. "I'll make sure you get on the list, Miss Grace."

I thanked him and then followed him back inside with a coy smile. Dylan was fast becoming my new best friend.

THIRTY

Tommy

As we left the studio I saw one of the assistants hand Piper something and whisper in her ear. The way he stared at her made my blood boil and my mind race. What had they been up to while I was on the set? I'd decided against public humiliation and gone with a close call instead, just enough to rile her up, and instead of being grateful it appeared she'd spent the time cozying up to the hired help.

"What did he want?" I demanded when I could finally get her alone.

"Nothing," she replied, grinning at me mischievously. Piper was playing games with me, and dangerous ones at that. That wasn't gonna fly.

"He handed you something, what was it?"

"A surprise…"

I let out a low growl. I didn't like surprises at all. "I'll tell you later. Well, more like show you."

Hmm, that sounded better. Had she arranged some kind of a date for us? I had to wonder. It wasn't like we were the dating type, but I figured we were slowly coming around. Perhaps it was also time to come clean about our relationship soon too? I had so many secrets swirling in the back of my mind and couldn't deny it'd be a relief to rid myself of one.

We went back to the hotel and it irked me when Piper refused my advances. It was late. I wanted to fuck and then fall asleep. But instead, she was getting changed into a skimpy black dress and kept telling me to put on my best suit.

After my dissatisfaction faded, my interest returned. Piper truly was intent on taking me out somewhere and so I did as she asked. I obliged her small trial of dominance and let her take the lead. It was only a half hour before we were back downstairs and climbing into a sleek black car she'd evidently hired for the occasion.

Piper stayed quiet as the driver took us to our destination, but as soon as we pulled up, I knew what to expect inside. This wasn't my first rodeo, even though it clearly seemed to be hers.

I didn't want her to make a fool out of herself so I took charge once she'd handed a piece of paper to the man on the door—presumably the same piece that boy had given her earlier—and he'd let us inside. It was just as I had expected. An underground S&M club catering for anyone from the fresh new types who were after just a little bit above vanilla to the hardcore pain fiends who wanted to either give it or take it at an extreme level.

"Why, Piper, you've outdone yourself," I whispered as we both took in the view. The place wasn't full by any means but it was well turned out and while people stopped and stared as we passed, none of them said a word. If they told their friends how they'd seen Tommy Darke and Piper Grace at an underground sex club they'd have to reveal their dark sexual habits in the process so I counted on their desire to remain out of the limelight to ensure we did the same.

"I told you I had a surprise for you," Piper told me when we came to a stop and watched a naked group of women who were casually playing with one another. Some were experimenting with nipple clamps and floggers, but I could tell they were either paid to be there or had been instructed on how to lure the lurkers in. There was no real spark between any of them. Not like if otherwise heterosexual women were touching another for the very first time. I wanted more than choreographed tantalization.

The sight still served its apparent purpose. I grew hard just thinking about how Piper would look with another woman's lips around her clit. Would she grow shy or would she grab her hair and pull her closer? I found myself wondering about it while watching her as she watched them.

"Will you let me have you, Piper? Here, in front of whoever wants to see?" I whispered in her ear. I relished in the sound as her breath hitched. She stared up at me with those doe eyes of hers and bit her bottom lip nervously as she considered her response.

"Would you hurt me or punish me?" she asked in response. My girl was learning. She had to know what she was getting herself into before committing and I loved how she was figuring out some of my intricacies at last. Piper knew I loved to torment her before tantalizing. Would she let me do it here? I couldn't tell. I decided to risk it.

"Yes," I said.

"How?" she replied, surprising me. Well at least it wasn't a no. I thought of the film I'd frequented and how I wanted to recreate it somehow. Could it be possible? I was willing to try if she was.

"I'd like to blindfold you. Make it so you can't see a thing as I take you in my hands and then spank you with them. Maybe worse." She stiffened, and rightly so. I hadn't really given her a full answer and we both knew how we were taking a risk being there at all, let alone if I started one of our punishment fuck sessions with a captive audience.

"Let me think about it," she answered and I nodded. Again, it wasn't a no.

I led her deeper into the club so we could take in the sights. It came as no surprise to me that it wasn't like you'd see in the movies or read about in books. Not everyone there was a glorious Adonis, nor did they all ooze money or sex appeal. They were simply everyday people with a combined interest in fucking partners who also wanted something more than a bit of missionary and then snuggles.

We watched one couple going at it who had to both be in their forties. His body wasn't bad and neither was hers given her age, but I was put off by the slapping sound they were making as they thrust together. Far different from the sound of leather meeting flesh, theirs was purely natural and an extreme turn off for me.

I took Piper into another room where we watched a dominatrix whip her submissive male lover as he cowered before her. Nothing about it made any sense to me, but Piper seemed intrigued and so we hovered there for a short while before I led her deeper into the dungeon. I wandered what scene we would happen upon next and found myself pleasantly surprised when we were presented with a woman who had been bound, gagged, and blindfolded. She was lying on a leather bed with her legs stretched open so that everyone could see every inch of her. She had nowhere to hide and the idea of strapping Piper to that same bed had me reaching for her.

"Can you imagine how she must be feeling?" I whispered in her ear. "Is she scared or anxious? Perhaps worried whether she looks good or is turning people on. Or does she like the attention?"

"I think she does," Piper replied, tilting her head up to look at me. "She's not shivering or trying to cover herself. Her breathing is even too, look." I did, noticing the same as Piper. The woman loved what was being done to her and wasn't about to put a stop to it anytime soon as far as

I could tell.

"How do you think you would feel in her place?"

Piper watched the couple for a moment and I could see her eyes going to the hard-on the man approaching was sporting. When he touched the woman, she flinched and he responded by pinching one of her nipples before forcing his way inside of her. Piper continued watching intently and I hoped she might be coming around to the idea of me doing the same to her one day.

"I think I'd feel vulnerable. But then I'd like it once you started to touch me. Especially when you made me feel good," she finally answered.

"And what about before that, when you'd be at my mercy?"

Piper shook her head.

"I'd be scared."

Damn, she had no idea what she did to me with words such as those. Rather than put me off, she simply spurred my dark desire forwards. I wanted nothing more than for her to spend an evening at my mercy having been scared and then pleasured in equal measure.

"Were you scared earlier when I told Washington how I came all over you on the set?"

"Yes," she replied with a laugh. "I also wanted to murder you."

My cock rocketed to life in my pants at hearing her say that. To even consider that she might be capable of that act had me wanting to bend her over and fuck her then and there. She couldn't know how what she'd said affected me. God, I was full of raw desire to not only take her, but to have another woman too. Not in the same way of course. No, Piper had all of me now, but I still wanted to try to recreate what Marina had given me. Could I do it when it wasn't spur of the moment? Was I capable of premeditated murder?

Yes, came the voice from deep within me. Yes. I was.

THIRTY-ONE

Piper

Tommy went so quiet I had to turn and properly look into his face to make sure he was okay. He seemed lost in thoughts. Away with them and chasing something I couldn't be sure he'd ever tell me about. When he snapped back to reality and grinned at me, my heart leapt, and not in a good way. What I saw was ruthless and cold. Like when you saw the mug shots of serial killers after the police had caught them. I went cold too, but in fear.

Something about this club had stirred up something inside of him. Something I was quite convinced I wasn't going to like.

"Let's get out of here," he groaned and for the first time, I didn't follow him. I didn't know what to expect when he got me alone and I was growing more fearful of what awaited me back at the hotel.

"Tommy," I whimpered when I finally stepped out of the room and caught up to him in the hallway. "I'm, urm… I'm not feeling great. It just came over me all of a sudden so I am gonna stay in my room tonight. Just in case I have the flu or something. I don't want to pass you my germs."

He didn't believe a word I was saying and tried to argue with me. He then resorted to pleading, but I stood my ground. I needed some space and wasn't going to change my mind. Eventually, Tommy seemed to realize he wasn't going to sway me so he conceded, even though I could see he hated it.

"Sure. Whatever. You go get some rest. I'll see you tomorrow," he said with a blank expression and I cringed. I'd expected him to leave with me, but he didn't. Tommy gave me a dark look of indifference and then sauntered back into the room we'd just left without so much as a backward glance in my direction.

Talk about a one-eighty. That guy was giving me whiplash with his ups and downs, but I figured I'd told him I was leaving and wanted to be alone so did just that. I called the driver and left without another word.

I went back to the room I'd barely touched since arriving in London because I'd spent my nights in Tommy's bed rather than my own. There, I busied myself by running a bath and then climbed into the hot suds with a sigh. It felt good to unwind after the hectic few weeks we'd been having and I let myself slide beneath the surface to soak my hair.

I stayed there for a few seconds, holding my breath, and a thought came to me. A feeling of wonder. Many, in fact. I wondered how it would feel to fade away. Would I be missed? Passed off as some kind of poor, overworked soul who'd fallen asleep in the tub and drowned? Or would there be stories circulating about me while questioning my morals? People from the club might come forward and tell the story of how I was there but seemed off and then had left in a hurry. And then that boy, Dylan, he might tell them what I'd said. And of course there was Tommy. Would he be incriminated?

I jumped up and out of the water. Tommy. What would he think if another woman close to him died in such a way? I was sure it would break him and there was no way I could do that. Even hypothetically, the thought of leaving him that way broke my heart.

My thoughts then naturally turned to Marina and what she'd done. I started to imagine her there, lying in her own blood until Tommy had found her. It must've been awful.

In a bid to get my mind onto something else, I grabbed the waterproof control and turned on a small television set that'd been built into the wall down by my feet. God, I loved posh hotels and their randomly awesome added features. I flicked around the channels for a while and stopped as soon as I saw a movie that was playing on one of them. A young Tommy Darke was on the screen depicting yet another of his shadier roles. The movie had to be about ten years old and yet he'd hardly aged at all. He was violently beating a young woman and his coldness made me shudder, but I also couldn't take my eyes off him. There was a glint in his eye I had seen before. Why was I drawn to the bad guy? Where was my sanity? I was glued to the screen and even as I continued to watch him sink further into darkness, I liked what I saw. I liked him. The name truly matched him perfectly.

I hit the information button and read the blurb. He was portraying a ruthless gangster for the first but not last time. This one seemed far worse than George, though. He enjoyed beating the woman I'd caught him with on screen, but then the strangest thing happened. She began to whimper, begging him to stop. He refused, which was when she started to cry.

Tommy—or whatever character he was playing—stopped dead and glowered at her with a horrified expression on his cruel face. He seemed disgusted with the girl for daring shed tears over what he was doing to her, but rather than discard her or send her away, his character murdered the poor girl in cold blood.

"You don't cry, Milly. Not in front of me. I told you, didn't I?" he then screamed at her lifeless body before spitting on her and then walking away with a growl.

My hand flew to my mouth. I knew it was just a movie and not real, but so much of it was scarily familiar. I recognized the actress and was sure she'd also had a number of hit movies since so was further reminded of how it was two actors playing out a scene. But it just felt so real.

It didn't take me long to realize why. I had seen that rage. I had felt those hands on me. But worst of all, I had been regarded with that same look of disgust. Tommy had told me himself how tears were a trigger for him and I'd seen what my own had done to him. Was his trigger even real? Had it come from him or from the character? I had to know for sure because if that trigger was actually part of a character profile gone rogue, then there was something a lot more dangerous about Tommy than I'd realized.

I grabbed my cell and leaned over the side of the tub with it as I loaded my search engine and typed in the name of the guy Tommy was playing in the movie. I needed to know if the crying thing had been written in because it was real and if so, for whom.

Johnny McIntyre was a man no one dared mess with. He had an aversion to women in general and not only called them weak to their faces, but repeatedly beat any who foolishly tried to get close to him. He became famous for strangling his own sister at the age of fifteen because, in his words, she did nothing but cry all the time. After that, Johnny brutally punished any woman who dared shed a tear in front of him…

I could read no more, but it didn't matter anyway. I'd seen more than enough to read between the blurred lines of Tommy's personality. He wasn't as brutal as this Johnny fellow, but damn could he be as cold. He had other traits that were uncannily similar to his other characters too.

I delved deeper over his movie history. As I read over his many movie hits and their plot summaries, I realized how so many of his roles had stayed with him. Like the hiker who had loved the solace of the mountains and was a skilled huntsman. Or the cocky playboy with a penchant for BDSM. And not to mention the manipulative drug lord who'd seduced women by drugging them and then brainwashing them.

They were all intense and had a dangerous side to them. And just like Tommy, they each hid it in front of everyone. But not the woman they loved. No, she was the only one who saw beneath the mask and had to live with what she found there. Because once she was under his skin, there seemed there was no way out.

I sympathized with each and every one of them. But I was different, wasn't I? This was real. Not a movie or a plot line someone had created, but my actual life. No one else had seen it or experienced first hand how it felt to have to make amends with Tommy's dark side. But I had. He'd readily shown me and I'd mistaken it for a bit of fun. But not any more. This was real and it was dangerous. I had to be careful otherwise God only knew what he might do to punish me if I ever truly hurt him.

THIRTY-TWO

Tommy

After months of tormenting myself and going back and forth with my emotions and conscience, I'd finally chosen which side of the coin I wanted to rule me. I'd been desperate to explore that side of myself and had struggled with my conscience about doing so with Piper. But then she'd walked away from that club and left me to play with my demons rather than wrestle with them any longer.

One of the many nameless, faceless girls from the dungeon was in my keep. I'd gone back to her apartment after the night was over and now had her tied up with her cunt on full display before me. She wanted me to fuck her so badly I could practically smell it. The whore was lifting her hips off the bed trying to entice my cock to fill her, but she wasn't getting anywhere near it. Instead, I decided to play a little longer. I took a mask from a travel pouch in her bedside unit and covered her eyes with it. Next, I used the earplugs that were also in the pack to block up her ears, rendering her both blind and deaf.

"Please," she whimpered, bucking against the restraints I'd put her in. "Please, master. Please fuck me."

I slapped her across the face and grinned as I saw the handprint I left behind. She didn't cry out and so I struck again. This time she let out a whimper and a sniffle that I presumed meant there were tears in her eyes. Thank fuck for the blindfold. At least that plan had worked.

After weighing up my options, I opted for checking out what else the girl had in her trusty bedside drawers and was pleasantly surprised by her array of toys and implements. I wasn't going to have sex with her myself, but this girl was certainly going to be fucked raw by the time I was done with her. I wanted to beat her, so I did.

First, I slapped her breasts. I then spanked her thighs and opened them wider, getting rougher and rougher every time I put my hands on her again. She had been trained to take it, and so I let my urges rule me. I did whatever I wanted, but only within reason. She was a masochist and could probably take more, but I had a reputation to uphold. A public persona to protect. She couldn't walk away in serious harm. And so after I was done, I gave her what she'd begged me for, but never with the real me. She didn't deserve that. Only Piper.

"Don't take off the mask until I've left," I ordered when I was done making her scream for me with both pleasure and pain. I was right to think I couldn't do anything more. It was too risky. I'd weighed up my options and knew people would've seen us leave together. There might also be surveillance cameras in her building or on the street outside showing me going up to her apartment. I would be caught if I indulged my murderer fantasy. If I was going to do it, I'd have to plan it meticulously in future, not on a whim.

"Thank you, master," she whimpered when I finally untied her.

I took a good look at my handiwork and took a mental picture. Her thighs and ass cheeks were red after my beatings and she let out a soft moan as I rubbed my hands over them soothingly. Aftercare was a big thing in this scene and I knew I had an obligation to make sure she was okay. Her ass still held the butt plug I'd filled it with and I left it in place. She could deal with that later. Her pussy was still full too. I'd found one of those double length dildos I'd seen lesbians use and had fucked her with it relentlessly. I could still see her clenching it from her final orgasm and carefully withdrew it. I wasn't sure if she'd known it wasn't my cock inside of her, but she hadn't asked and I didn't feel much like volunteering the info. I'd let her believe whatever she wanted to and didn't give a fuck what she assumed had happened between us.

Our time was over. I had to get back to the hotel and finally get my own rocks off. Piper had asked for privacy and she'd gotten it, for a few hours at least. I was about to burst her little bubble, and God help her if she tried to refuse me.

THIRTY-THREE

Piper

I woke with a start and looked around, finding nothing but the blackout darkness in my room. I began to wish I'd put on a little light somewhere before falling asleep, but I'd left my bath in such a tired state that all I'd wanted to do was crawl into bed and get comfortable. I'd been asleep moments later.

It was nothing, I told myself. Just a noise outside or someone out in the hallway. That was it. I had to be imagining things and managed to convince myself it was my mind playing tricks on me. I hadn't sleep alone in weeks either so was probably just on edge.

I turned onto my side towards the center of the bed and nestled back into the pillows, which was when I heard the footsteps approaching the bed. I stiffened for a split second and then told myself to run, or at the very least fight back.

By the time the covers were thrown off my naked body and I was exposed on the bed, I'd clambered up and was halfway turned, ready to do whatever I could to fend off whoever had snuck into my room in the dead of night. It was no use. He knew exactly where to strike me. His flattened palm hit me directly in the center of my chest and the air rushed out of my lungs.

I fell back, gasping for breath while my attacker quickly disrobed and then spread my legs. I hoped to God it was Tommy. I was going to be furious with him, of course, but at least if it was Tommy I could handle being manhandled and tossed around like this. At least with Tommy I kinda liked his heavy-handedness. At least with Tommy I could let myself enjoy the consensual non-consent of it all.

"Stay down," he told me when I'd caught my breath and tried to squirm away. That was when I knew for sure it was him. I'd know that voice anywhere and even with the doubts about his sanity still plaguing me, my carnal instincts took over. I wanted him and it was clear he wanted me too, but if we were playing this game then I was going to properly go for it. I kicked him in the ribs when he got closer and, judging by his deep grunt, I had caught him nicely off guard. When I kicked again he caught my ankle right before my foot connected with his chest.

I expected him to push it outwards and open my legs again, but instead he pushed it towards me, along with the other foot he had also grabbed while he was immobilizing me. Before I knew it my knees were up by my ears, my ass and pussy facing the ceiling. Tommy knew how flexible I was thanks to the yoga so didn't stop pushing me and soon my hips were crushing against my stomach, which resulted in my stomach crushing my lungs.

I tried to push back but felt my strength waning thanks to the lack of oxygen. I thought I might pass out and was about to croak out a plea when Tommy climbed over me and plunged his cock inside of my pussy. He began pounding in and out, each plunge twisting me further in on myself, and at first I was struggling, but it wasn't long before the discomfort turned into pleasure. Like always, he overpowered me and did whatever the hell he wanted and, like always, I let him.

By the time we'd both climaxed and he let me go, I knew that despite the things I thought I'd learned about him, it'd would never change what was going on between the pair of us. It didn't matter the doubts I had or the questions that'd plagued me while lazing in that tub. I wasn't prepared to ask him about them or demand to know the truth and until I was, I was doomed to forever wonder if I truly knew the man I'd fallen in love with.

I also had to wonder if I should cut my losses and run, but knew I was too scared to run from him. Too scared to be without him. Tommy owned me now and there was nothing I could do about it.

THIRTY-FOUR

Tommy

Piper was huddling against her pillow by the time I'd finished with her and while I knew she wasn't happy with what I'd done, I refused to pander to her girlish whims and apologize. Thanks to the darkness of the room I didn't have to see her face so brought no attention to her soft whimpering. I was sure to hold her though, spooning her from behind. I even marveled at my ability to know she was upset and not let her get to me. Perhaps I was finally overcoming my obsessive aversion to the sight of tears? Or could it just be hers I was becoming untroubled by? Maybe not.

The main problem was that I didn't feel sorry for what I'd done. I'd used my keycard and invaded her private space even when she'd asked for a night by herself. I'd forced myself on her and crushed her body beneath mine so that she had no hope of fighting me back. Not a chance in hell of stopping me. And I'd loved every second of it.

That girl from the club had twisted me up so tightly that I'd been fit to burst and was surprised I'd even managed to last long enough for Piper to reach her orgasm.

As I listened to her tears slow, so did her breathing. I then felt her body calm and drift into sleep, and I tried to switch off but couldn't. All I could think about was that girl and how I'd wanted to take things further. Do more than just beat her.

I decided I needed some air so sneaked out of bed and pulled on my clothes. Piper didn't so much as stir as I crept away and soon I was back out in the dim lights of the hallway.

Rather than go down to my own room I headed for the stairs and followed them down and out a door at the bottom. There, I found myself standing out the back of the hotel and I didn't know what to do with myself or where to go.

That was when I saw him. There was a young man kneeling behind one of the dumpsters and I could see the tourniquet around the top of his arm from my vantage point a few yards away. Fucking junkie. I approached cautiously, watching him as he watched me.

"Hey, back off man," he croaked but I simply slid down beside him.

"I'm not here for your stash, pal. Just checking you're okay."

"I'm fine," he said with a hiss as he pushed the needle filled with dirty brown shit into his vein. With a sigh he let his head fall back against the grimy bins and his hand fall to the side, the needle clattering against the concrete floor. I reached for it on instinct but was sure to cover my hand with my hoodie when I did. There was still some heroin inside and I leaned forward, spying how there was more left on the guy's bent spoon as well.

Desire overwhelmed me. A need so strong I knew I was a slave to it. A willing accomplice. So, I refilled the syringe, not even bothering to tap the air bubbles away, and then injected him with a second dose. He jumped at first, but was too out of it to react before he let out another sigh and his head rolled to one side, his lids closed.

I listened as his breathing became shallower and shallower and was beyond calm the entire time, even when he slipped away and stopped breathing completely. I watched him turn blue and even risked a closer look once I was sure he'd died. It was a curious sight, but one that fascinated me. Not as much as seeing a woman in the relative stages of death, but still interesting all the same.

And then, as though nothing was amiss, I put the needle back in the boy's hand and walked away. I was sure to keep in the shadows for as long as possible before then circling around and going back inside. The little junkie would be found before too long and while this time around I knew there was nothing to link me with him, I was sure to head back to Piper's room to ensure I had an alibi.

As I lay there beside her, all I could think was how I'd done it again. Not the same and certainly not as exciting or satisfying, but I'd done it. I'd killed someone. That made two people now and I knew then and there how I wasn't stopping at that. I'd do it again. Hopefully more and more. Next time I would have a woman at my mercy like the girl from the club, but instead of untying her and leaving, I would slit her throat. Or squeeze it shut. Yes, that'd be good. To feel it crushing beneath my hands.

Damn, I was hard again. I grabbed my cock and started jerking off, the images so clear in my mind of what I had done and what I still wanted to do. I took myself close to the edge of my release and then stopped. It just wasn't good enough.

I curled my body around Piper's and teased the head of my cock inside her from behind. She stirred but didn't wake so I pushed myself the rest of the way in and came. My darling girl had no idea and I guessed she'd been so exhausted from my visit earlier that night she'd fallen into such a deep sleep and hadn't felt me penetrate her. I left my cock where it was until it'd gone down and then I withdrew.

A quick clean up with a tissue and I was ready to catch some zzz's, so I turned away and closed my eyes. Sleep came to me quickly and it was full of the best dreams. Girls lined up ready for me to fuck them and then kill them. I did it over and over again and always with the same 'service with a smile' approach. Each of them were nameless and faceless, but they all screamed for me as they came and then screamed the same way as they died. It was heaven.

Of course, I woke the next morning with another raging boner and I turned over to find Piper lying exactly where I'd left her. I nestled right back into position and starting pushing myself inside. She groaned and tried to pull away, but I grabbed her hips and tucked another couple of inches into place. I could feel her tensing around me, resisting the intrusion, but it was no use. I had her exactly where I wanted her and was going to take what was mine.

"I'm sore from last night," she whimpered as I began rocking back and forth, my cock only coming out an inch or so rather than me fucking her the full length at a time.

"I'll be gentle," I replied as I pushed her onto her stomach and lifted her ever so slightly so that her ass and cunt were on full display as I climbed up on top of her. Piper whimpered as I began going for it but she didn't tell me to stop and I soon felt her begin to melt. She grew wetter around my cock and stopped fighting. She didn't even struggle when I licked one finger to moisten it and pushed it inside her ass. I couldn't help myself. It was far too appealing just sitting there on show and looking all inviting. She relaxed around me and that told me she'd done it before, so I slid in a second and began teasing her open, ready to accept my cock.

I didn't even ask. I simply withdrew from her pussy and plunged it into the hole above. Piper moaned into her pillow but still didn't fight, and I could see her hands gripping the bed beneath as I began sliding in and out.

Again, she didn't stop me. I took her compliance as invitation and went for it, savoring every second I was inside of that sweet, tight hole. She soon came for me and I quickly followed, emptying into her ass without a care before slowly retreating.

Piper ran for the bathroom before I could even check her over and a second later I could hear her using the facilities. "Are you okay?" I asked, thinking I'd better at least check.

Did I care? I thought so, but wasn't overly sure at the same time. She was becoming something so wonderful to me. So… what was the word? Compliant? Perhaps. Piper was in a place where she did everything I wanted her to do and didn't fight me. Not since the day at the cabin when she'd learned how much joy I truly took from watching her squirm and wilt under the pressure of my humiliating tactics.

I heard no response so opened the door and walked right on in. Piper flushed bright red and grasped in horror that I'd found her sitting on the toilet.

"Tommy!" she cried, but I refused to leave. Instead I turned on the shower and climbed right on in. After a second I poked my head out of the curtain and shot Piper a cool grin.

"You think I didn't know you'd have to squeeze my cum out? This isn't my first ride up the a-train," I told her, relishing in Piper's embarrassment.

"Doesn't mean you have to be here while I do it," she groaned, wiping herself and then flushing the toilet.

I put out my hand.

"Come here," I demanded. She hesitated for just a second and then did as I'd asked. I was glad, but also angry that there was even any hesitation at all. However, I let it slide. For now.

Piper climbed in with me and I grabbed the soap and got to work on her pussy and asshole. She tried to stop me but I was having none of it. I didn't go inside, nor was I rough, and soon she was putty in my hands. Piper welcomed my aftercare and let me trail suds all over her tender parts and when I washed them away, she even let me shave her completely bald from her pubic bone to her coccyx. Then, with her legs wide I inspected my handiwork while the shower water thundered down onto us like rain. I parted her lips and licked my way from her clit to her pussy and then I slid a finger inside. I knew she wasn't ready for me to fuck her again so simply fingered my way in and out while teasing her clit with my tongue. My girl came for me hard and by the time I'd finished, she had a fire in her eyes that drove me wild.

We switched places and Piper cleaned me up before sliding her mouth over my shaft and then forcing it to the back of her mouth. It was heaven and I let myself moan and groan with pleasure as she licked and sucked me to the brink of another orgasm. But then, she stopped.

With a cunning grin Piper then stood over me and turned around. I was now lying on the floor of the bath and watched as she started to lower herself over me. I figured it was time for a sixty-niner but it appeared she had other plans. Her soreness either abated or ignored, Piper pushed me inside her pussy and began to ride me. Reverse-cowgirl had never really been my thing before, but with Piper taking charge, I would happily be her steed and she could ride me all day long.

I held my orgasm back and got a second wind as she arched her hips and moved back and forth atop me. I watched the muscles in her body contract and move with skilled precision and couldn't get enough. When she came again it was a surprise to both of us and I could see her strength wane in the aftermath so let myself go.

Like a jackrabbit I pushed up and down into her until I shot my load. She was trembling by the time she'd climbed free and I watched her with fascination as she once again tried to hide her modesty from me as she clambered to the toilet and took a piss. From my vantage point I could see it pouring out of her and refused to look away. "You're so fucking beautiful," I told her and loved the smile Piper was overcome with.

She then started to giggle.

"Even when royally fucked and taking a piss?"

"Especially then."

THIRTY-FIVE

Piper

Tommy finished taking his shower while I shoved on a robe and headed back towards the bedroom to grab the room service menu in readiness to order some breakfast. I also snatched the remote from the center table and turned on the TV set, where I found an array of morning television shows to choose from. I stopped as soon as I saw Tommy's face plastered all over one of them and turned up the volume.

"After reports that he visited an underground sex club last night, Hollywood star and movie bad boy, Tommy Darke was allegedly seen leaving with one of the other club visitors. In the aftermath of her night of passion with the notoriously private star his lover has agreed to sell her story to the highest bidder and went on record today as promising a sex story worthy of rivaling any you might've heard before. There's been no response from Tommy or his people, but we look forward to hearing both sides of the apparently sordid tale of BDSM and so much more. It looks like a certain someone is going to have to either answer to or accept his new reputation as a ladykiller…"

I went cold. He'd gone home with another woman and

given her the night of her life? And then he'd come to my room and had sex with me too? I wanted to throw up or scream the place down, but opted instead to slump into the nearest chair.

I felt lost. Why hadn't I listened to myself before when I knew something was wrong? It had to be that I was blinded for my love for Tommy. There was no other explanation. Had he manipulated me? Brainwashed me somehow? It seemed the most logical reason for how I'd been acting and how often I had given him the benefit of the doubt when I ought not to have. When I'd covered for him and let him get away with hurting me because he'd convinced me it was all part of something I had brought to life within him. That his darkness was somehow my fault. My burden to bear.

All of my instincts had slowly become wired to his actions. His ideas had seemed to mirror my own, but now that I was thinking about it more clearly, it was the other way around. I was mirroring him because he had gotten under my skin and influenced me into complying. Made me think it was my idea when he was the puppet master all along.

He'd broken me beyond repair. Taken my body and my heart, as well having forced me to give up my freedom and free will because he'd infiltrated my mind and made me trust him. Tommy had manipulated me to believe the lies he'd woven between us while molding me into his perfect and willing slave.

But not any more. My eyes were wide open and I could see him for what he truly was. A monster. A master manipulator who was nothing but a fake smile and pretend promises. What I had discovered the night before was true. Each side of his personality was a ruse. A pretense so that all the world wouldn't see him for what he really was. But I could finally see.

Everything I thought I knew about Tommy was a lie. Was the man I thought I knew just another role he'd been playing? I believed so, and had to presume it had been the same his adult life.

I grabbed my cell and checked out the online gossip pages. His name was everywhere. His face splattered over every one of them as they speculated about what'd happened between him and that woman. There wasn't so much as a mention of me having been at the club too and I breathed a sigh of relief for that one fact, but the rest of it made my blood boil.

How could Tommy do that to me? How could he be so incredibly callous and vile? I knew how. Because everything I thought he was and everything I thought he felt for me was a lie. A cruel, cruel myth he'd let me believe ever since that day in his goddamn swimming pool.

Tommy sauntered out of the bathroom without a care in the world, but then saw for himself how he was today's top story and I couldn't say he even looked sorry for what he'd done.

"I want you to leave, Tommy. Get out of my room and don't ever come back," I told him in a cold voice I knew was purely for show. There was no I way I was truly that calm. Underneath the surface I was losing my shit and knew it wasn't long until the façade would shatter along with my heart.

He frowned at me and then started to laugh, shaking his head.

"I didn't fuck her. I just roleplayed a little to satisfy some kinks I've been thinking about doing with you. I just shoved a dildo in her cunt a few times to make her think I was doing the deed. You know I'd never be with anyone but you now, Piper. I love you."

I couldn't believe he was daring to shrug off the story. That he was genuinely amused by my pain. I could tell by the stupid grin on his face that he truly thought he'd done no wrong. That I was being silly by letting it upset me.

I stood and glared at him. The mask really had now fallen and I saw the real him. The man I'd been trying to deny was there all along. The monster. Not the person I thought I loved.

He truly believed in what he was saying. Honestly looked surprised that I had the audacity to call him out on what he considered to be reasonable behavior.

"You need to leave, Tommy," I tried again. "We're done. Do you hear me? Done!"

"You don't mean that," he tried, but I wasn't going to surrender to him. Not anymore. Not ever again. "You're just angry. Let's talk about this."

"I don't want to talk to you. I don't want to look at you. Now, get the fuck out of my room before I call security," I demanded, my voice turning shrill.

His smile dropped in a heartbeat and he charged towards me. I did my best not to show him any fear, but couldn't hide it when he fixed me with that awful stare of his. The one that meant I was going to incur his wrath. But it didn't matter anymore, because he wasn't going to be anywhere near me to deliver one of his fucked-up punishments ever again. I meant it when I'd said I wanted him to go away.

"You don't get to decide we're over," he ground. "We're done when I say so, Piper. I own you."

I slapped him across the face with all the strength I could muster and then quickly stepped back, realizing I'd made a rash choice and potentially huge mistake in doing so. He was unpredictable. And dangerous. And I'd just acted out rashly.

Tommy responded by picking up a nearby armchair as if it weighed nothing at all before then throwing directly at the still blaring TV set. The force of the throw ruined them both and all I could do was stand there in shock and dismay.

"No one owns me," I eventually whimpered. "Least of all someone like you, Tommy Darke. You're a fraud and I know I won't even miss you, because I don't think I ever really knew you. Now get the fuck away from me." I went over to the door and opened it wide, hoping he'd just do as he'd been asked and leave me the hell alone.

He moved toward me in slow strides, his face seeming contorted and bereft after his outburst, and came to a stop beside me. I watched as every expression and emotion then disappeared from his face, leaving nothing but an utterly blank canvas. All I saw was darkness. And cold, cold eyes that I knew were the window to his empty soul.

I had been right about everything.

"If I don't have you, I'll do it again and again. I won't be able to stop myself," he told me, his voice barely more than a hoarse whisper.

"You should've thought about that before you cheated on me with that whore," I replied. "Do it again, for all I care. Do it over and over again while you think of me and realize what you've lost. I hope you die alone, Tommy. I hope no one ever dares to love you again because I know now that you're not capable of love."

He walked out of my life that day and while it broke me, I hoped that would be the end of my love affair with Tommy Darke. I longed for the day that I could forget him and carry on with my life. But I also feared that I might never truly be free. No matter what lay ahead, he'd infected me and I somehow knew that to some extent, I would always be Tommy's Girl.

To be concluded in part two…

ABOUT THE AUTHOR

Laura started her writing career putting together short stories and fan fiction, usually involving her favourite movie characters caught up in steamy situations, and wrote her first full length novel in 2013. A self-confessed computer geek, Laura enjoys both the writing and creative side of her journey, and regularly seeks out the next big gadget on her wish list to help facilitate those desires.

She spends her days with her husband, two children and their cocker spaniel Milo, as well as making the most of her free time by going to concerts with her friends, or else listening to rock music at home while writing (a trend many readers may have picked up on in her stories.)

If you enjoyed this book, please take a moment to share your thoughts by leaving a review to help promote Laura's work.

Laura Morgan's novels include:

The Black Rose series:
When Darkness Falls: A Short Prequel to the Black Rose series (Permanently FREE)
Embracing the Darkness: book #1 in the Black Rose series
A Slave to the Darkness: book #2 in the Black Rose series
Forever Darkness: book #3 in the Black Rose series
Destined for Darkness: book #4 in the Black Rose series
A Light in the Darkness: book #5 in the Black Rose series
Don't Pity the Dead, Pity the Immortal: Novella #1
Two Worlds, One War: Novella #2

And her contemporary romance novels:
Forever Lost (gangster/crime)
Forever Loved (gangster/crime follow on from Forever Lost)
Rough Love (MC crime/mystery story. Can be read as a stand-alone)
Fly Away – (A short romance story – probably Laura's sweetest story to date!)
Ensnared – A dark romance (Permanently FREE via Laura's webpage)

Laura also writes Science Fiction under the alias LC Morgans, with her new novels:
Humankind: Book 1 in the Invasion Days series
Autonomy: Book 2 in the Invasion Days series
Resonant: Book 3 in the Invasion Days series
Hereafter: Book 4 in the Invasion Day series

36580195R00111

Printed in Great Britain
by Amazon